Single No More

Jennifer Goodman

DEDICATION

To my supportive family who encouraged me to write.
Thank you, Stephanie, for reading it and liking it.

Single No More

Chapter One

"Cut!" Claire pushed back from the monitor she had been watching intently. "Hold on everyone, I have an idea." Everyone on set remained in place. She looked at her watch and then looked at the sky. She could see that the sunset was approaching, and with those clouds on the horizon, it would be gorgeous. This was a bonus.

"Okay people, I hadn't expected these clouds. This sunset is going to blow us away. We are going to use it. Mark, I want you to pan back and forth from the sunset to Ann and Zack for the duration. Back and forth, back and forth. You are the best at this. Use your instinct."

Mark saluted from his perch on camera 3 about 20 feet away from the couple. "Yes, ma'am. I got this."

"Sid, can you move left a bit so that the sunset

will be to the left of frame? And Terry, same for you on the right? Alice, be ready...we may need more lighting. Everyone else hold for five." Claire stood up to a chorus of "yes ma'ams," and walked across the grass toward the couple standing near the edge of the cliff. This really was a beautiful place. She had chosen this villa because it was remote, but not far from the city. And it wasn't really a cliff, per se; just a really steep incline down beyond the flat space of grass and wildflowers where they all stood. It looked like a cliff from the camera vantage point. The ocean was about 10 miles away, but from camera 3 it looked like it was right beyond the "cliff." That was the goal. Make it look beachy without the wind and the salt-air spray that made everyone's hair frizzy. Cindy, her make-up and hair genius, had already thanked her 5 separate times.

"Hey, lovebirds. Keep the emotion coming. I know it's not hard," She winked at them as they smiled back. Did she see tears in Ann's eyes already? "We are going to wait about 5 minutes and then start over. I think the sunset will be spectacular because of the clouds. The shot will be magical, not that you both need it. You are creating your own magic, right?" Ann and Zack both nodded furiously, and Ann blushed as she beamed up at Zack. "Ann, try to look surprised, K?" Claire reminded. Ann continued her nodding.

As Claire walked back to her chair, she threw a thumbs-up to her crew and they answered with their own versions of the gesture. Best crew on the planet, she thought, smiling, as she got settled into her chair and watched the monitor.

"Quiet on set!" Claire nodded to her intern. He walked into frame with the open clapperboard, looked at the camera and said, "Single No More, Cycle 12, Proposal Scene, Take 2," and snapped it closed.

Chapter 2

"CUT!" Claire declared, beaming, and jumped out of her chair, wiping her eyes awkwardly. "That was AMAZING!"

The crew knew better than to stop rolling. They had strict instructions to continue filming even after Claire "stopped" the scene. That was mostly for the contestants anyway. When they didn't think the camera was rolling, they did and said so many great things: natural things that Claire could use during editing. She was masterful. The rest of the crew cheered and clapped as Sid and Terry backed away from Ann and Zack a little, but kept their cameras trained on the couple. They were still kissing and hugging and laughing. This was the best part. Terry wiped a tear away from her face quickly as she backed away. She heard Sid sniff. When the camera operators got together, they always agreed that the last scene was the best. It was why they loved their jobs. Claire was a natural director, and they all loved her, but watching two people discover each other and then honestly declare their love for each other, was priceless. Claire had a way of orchestrating the whole story so that the raw honesty and emotion was never faked. She was a genius.

It was quickly getting dark, and so Ann and Zack headed to the waiting limousine that would take them to their new lives together. Once the limo started moving, Claire yelled, "Great work, everyone! Two more singles NO MORE" and wrapped the scene by drawing circles in the sky with her right hand and closing it in a fist. It was her personal cue to the camera crew to actually stop filming. High fives were shared all around and everyone started breaking down and packing up. Maggie ran up to her with her water and protein bar.

"Okay, boss, now eat." Maggie handed Claire the protein bar. It was already unwrapped and ready.

"Wow, I didn't realize I was hungry till now." Claire took two quick bites and a downed about half of the water bottle.

"I know. You never think of eating." Maggie sighed. "If I wasn't here, what would you do?

"Probably starve," Claire smirked as she chewed, "without even realizing it."

"I think you would probably figure it out at some point." Maggie looked at her clipboard as they started walking past the house and down the hill toward the vans. "You have that dinner with your brother tonight. Are you going to put him off again?"

"How many times have I rescheduled?"

"Do I have to keep track of that, too?" Maggie looked at her sideways and rolled her eyes.

Claire stopped walking and made a big, dramatic show of exasperation. "Aren't you supposed to do EVERYTHING?"

Maggie continued walking down the path and they both laughed as Claire started walking to keep up. Maggie was trying to make light of it, but she was worried about why Claire kept putting James off.

"No, really, Claire. Am I confirming? Or rescheduling?"

"Uhhh...I think I want to reschedule because I'm tired. This shoot wiped me out."

"Nope. Don't believe you. Shoots invigorate you. You lie like a rug. Why are you avoiding James? Just tell me. Maybe I can help." Maggie crossed her fingers, hoping for a straight answer this time. She liked James too much to keep calling with bad news. Even though she'd like to keep calling him...

Claire tried not to smile. But Maggie had caught her. Maggie Hendrick was not only the best personal assistant on the planet, she was Claire's best friend. How could she skate through this conversation without talking about the obvious?

The inevitable. The subject she hated most. Ironic isn't it, she thought. I make a living helping others fall in love and I'm really good at it, but I can't deal with the thought of it for myself. Blah blah blah. MY life does NOT imitate art.

After a moment of silence as they got to her car, Claire blurted out, "He wants to set me up with a friend of his. And. I. Don't. Want. Too…. OKAY?"

"What?...Really?... That's why you have rescheduled SIX dinners with him?" Maggie started giggling.

"Stop laughing or you're fired." Claire declared; stone faced. "This is definitely NOT funny…wait…has it really been six???"

Maggie tried to contain the giggling, but it was an obvious struggle. She knew very well that the subject of dating was touchy with Claire, and the irony was pretty obvious.

"Stop it, now." Claire was also struggling not to laugh now. "No, really. Knock it off. Stop. Stop it… off," she stuttered.

"Stop it… off? Maggie sputtered through her laughter. "That's a good one. I'm going to start using it. C'mon girl, spill it. James wouldn't randomly fix you up. He knows better. He's the one who originally introduced you to Karl, the butthead."

"We aren't talking about Karl, but you are right. James knows how I feel. That is why I'm in avoid-mode. It scares me that he would try again. There must be something about this guy that James thinks is... safe? I've been fighting with myself for weeks about this. I've finally gotten over Karl. I don't think about it even remotely anymore. I'm safe. I'm happy with my life. I don't want to mess with that. I don't want to mess with my happiness right now."

"Happiness?" Maggie stared. "All you do is work and sleep? How is that happiness?"

"It's my happiness." Claire glared over the car at Maggie. "And I like it."

They both got in the car and Claire turned to Maggie. "Look Mags. I know that my life looks pitiful to you. I do. I know this. But I am comfortable. I like not having to explain why I do things. I like that no one complains when I eat my dinner in front of the TV, or that I don't cook, or that I don't like to exercise. I try to reserve a little bit of hope that I could find a guy who could love me and like me at the same time. But I don't know. Karl always said he loved me, but there were so many things about me that he didn't like. I wasn't this. I wasn't that. He wished I was more.... Blah blah blah. I like that no one is judging my every move anymore."

With that final statement, she started the car and backed up. Maggie struggled with what to say next. She agreed with Claire that Karl was awful. How should she argue Claire's logic?

Claire interrupted Maggie's thoughts, "Plus, James says he's an ACTOR." She said this with such venom. Such disgust. "Well, an out-of-work actor.

So, it's no one we know."

Woah, Maggie thought. No wonder. She knew well enough that Claire thought actors were self-absorbed and thoughtless. That was why she chose to work in the reality TV industry. She could work with real people and teach them how to be natural in front of the camera. Maggie could tell Claire was waiting for a lecture on being open to her true love. She decided that now was not the time.

"So, not only is he a guy, but he's an actor. Double strike." Maggie offered in mock horror, as she tried to lighten the mood.

Claire laughed. It was working. They drove a few miles in silence.

Claire turned to Maggie at a stop light. "So, you aren't going to tell me to go meet this guy?

"Nope," Maggie answered. "Not if he's an actor."

Chapter 3

Maggie got to work "rescheduling" the dinner with James, and Claire dropped her off at the studio so she could get her car.

Claire felt a little guilty that she wasn't calling James herself, but she knew that if she called, he would figure out a way to talk her into it, and then she would lose that battle. Nope, she was going home to sit in front of her TV and happily eat some frozen food—ice-cream included. That was that.

Her phone lit up. It was a text from Mags confirming that James was rescheduled to next weekend, and that Monday they would finalize the next "single" for the show. There were 10 guys in the running at this point and Claire liked to have her team narrow the list down to 3 for her to meet. She didn't like the chore of weeding through the hundreds of applicants they received every cycle, but she liked the option of choosing the guy she would work closely with for 6 weeks. Choosing the girls for the show was a different story. They used a computer algorithm to match the hundreds of girls who applied to the guy's profile. So, after choosing the new guy, the computer nerds would go to work asking him question after question to build his profile so that the 10 girls who get on the show actually have things in common with him. His choice is harder on the show, but ultimately compatible to him.

This system had never failed her. She still got Christmas cards from the couples who found each other on Single No More. She was proud of what she had accomplished.

Chapter 4

"Look dude, your sister obviously doesn't want to meet me." Andy said as he finished off his fourth slice of pizza. "We gotta stop eating pizza like this. I'm gaining." He patted his belly ruefully.

"True, we can't put it away like we used to." James patted his own belly in solidarity. "Well, I told you there was no way she would willingly go on a blind date even if I was the arranger." He said matter-of-factly. "This was why we had to have a plan B."

"And I'm not so comfortable with plan B. You know that, right? I'm not 100% sure this is the way."

James clapped Andy on the back. "You've got this. You are an actor, right? If you want to meet my sister," he pointed to the beaming photo of Claire on the wall, "you need to ACT. You need to bring it." James took the picture off the wall and handed it to Andy. "For inspiration."

"Tell me again what happens if I get there, and I don't feel it. You know...what if don't feel that connection to her? I look at her face in the picture and I'm just drawn to her, but what if that doesn't translate to real life?" Andy looked genuinely concerned. "And if I don't feel it, and they choose me for the show...What then?"

James got serious. "Then you just go after one of the girls they throw at you, man. Really, the fact that you are this sensitive about this makes me even more convinced that my sister would like you. You would be good for her, and she for you. The fact that this meeting will be less than honest is a bit of a worry, but we can always blame it on me and the fact that she refused to meet you otherwise. We can pretend to blame it on her being stubborn."

Andy got serious. "Really, James. She sounds like she really doesn't want to meet someone. Maybe we should just leave her alone. I'm not liking this."

James laughed. "You have come this far. You are a finalist, right? You will meet her on Monday, no matter what, and you can decide." He then added, "And remember that you cannot come off as an actor. You didn't put any of that on your application, right? That would kill it. She *hates* actors. You have to be real."

Andy laughed nervously, "And so why will she like me? This has been my question all along,

James. If she hates actors, what happens when I come clean and tell her that I endured Wall Street for 8 years, and I hated it? Acting is what I'm good at."

"You will get her with your loving, unselfish, gallant personality."

Andy threw a pillow at him.

Chapter 5

Andy had a hard time deciding what to wear to the "meet." That is the word the girl used. Like it wasn't an audition. Did they think it softened the blow? Made it less frightening? He wasn't that fooled. It's another audition. He had already breezed past the first two "meets" with flying colors. He was good looking. He had been told that, anyway. He didn't really pay attention. A girlfriend in college told him once that if you weren't concerned with whether or not you were attractive, that meant that you were. Attractive, that is. What did that mean? He guessed, maybe, that meant that he had never missed out on anything because he wasn't attractive enough? Whatever. He didn't think about it much. He just thought he was average.

He had blue eyes and dark brown hair that was thick enough to be curly if it got too long. He had thought, briefly, about seeing what it would be like long, but didn't want to endure the scruffy, in-between stage. He kept it short on the sides and a little longer on top. He was tall without being a sequoia, and he never worried about weight. His mom always bragged that he was blessed with a fast metabolism. He counted himself lucky because he disliked exercising. He'd tried every type, but couldn't stick with one. My poor heart will have to deal with it, he had decided. Exercising is a lonely endeavor. Football in high school was his only foray into the world of working out, and that was only marginally fun because there were always dozens of guys doing it with you.

He would meet Claire today. He was nervous. Not so much about making the show, but about meeting her. She was gorgeous and successful and totally against meeting someone. He admitted to himself that the latter was probably the biggest reason he was nervous. He knew from James that she had sworn off love in her life. Some idiot had mistreated her, and even though he had never met her, he was angry with the guy for treating her poorly. Who does that? What macho idiot has the nerve to make a woman feel bad about herself?

He decided on jeans and a blue button-down shirt with a pattern. He had been told his eyes pop when he wears blue. Well then, blue it is. I need all the pop I can get. I hope jeans aren't too casual, he thought.

He looked at the picture of Claire that James

gave him for inspiration. She had his same hair color and green eyes. He had no idea how tall she was or if she was skinny or fat. He didn't care. Her eyes spoke to him. He felt a little creepy having her picture in his possession without her knowledge. He made a mental note to give it back to James ASAP. He would see her in an hour and have a living picture after that.

Chapter 6

Claire brushed her hair behind her ears and bit at her lower lip. She was looking at the folios of the 3 finalists for the show. She was meeting them in 15 minutes. They would all be in the room together. She thought this way was best. She liked to watch them interact with each other and with her team to see who was a gentleman and who was more competitive. Their true personalities would emerge amid the stress of seeing their competition for the spot. She wished she had a huge one-way mirror like they use in interrogation rooms so she could just watch without their knowledge, but that would be unfair, probably. Anyway, the studio didn't have a large mirror like that and if she requested one, she guessed the unions might get nervous.

She read the names of the finalists while she looked at their photos. Drake Nelson, Mike

Albretti, Andrew Parker. They were all cute. They were always cute. TV didn't like otherwise. It was a sad reality. TV judged the book by its cover. It was that simple.

They were all looking for love. Looking for their soulmate. Looking for their perfect match. Whichever way you chose to say it, they were ready. Or they would have to be. At least that was how they would spin it on the show. They would have to choose an angle and sell it. The guy they chose would have to come up with his own mantra. His own belief statement. And even though she didn't believe it for herself, she still believed that everyone else deserved to find love. So even though her approach at first was always a little jaded and pessimistic, the guy would always change her mind with his behavior toward the girls he fell for. And there were always multiple girls, which made for bigger drama on screen. Each "single" she had worked with ended up falling for more than one of the girls on the show and would come crying to Claire off camera about how he was finding it impossible to choose. The angst was real. She always felt it. She would always try to orchestrate situations where the girls would show their true colors so it would be easier to choose. She tried to make it as natural as it could be with cameras rolling. It was different every season, depending on the participants. But, ultimately, watching two people discover each other was inspiring.

She usually had a favorite girl by the third episode. And, with only one exception, her favorite always got the ring. She couldn't explain that, and had never told anyone else that statistic. She wondered if it was because she got to know the guy so well through the computer match up phase, that she could see it before he did, or if it was because she watched all the film during editing.

Claire continued to study the photos. Which one will it be?

Chapter 7

"Nice to meet you, Andrew," Claire shook his hand and looked him straight in the face. She smiled a little and tilted her head slightly to one side, and it put him completely at ease. He wasn't nervous anymore. She was right in front of him and he was not nervous. What the heck? Shouldn't he be terrified? Her touch was electrifying. She let go of his hand and moved to the next guy. No wait, come back...stay with me, Andy thought.

As she moved toward guy #3, she clenched her hand to make the electric feeling go away. What was that? She thought. The one named Andrew had looked right into her soul. Did she know him? Had she met him before today? She mentally shook her head. Get it together, girl. He was cuter in person. Drop dead gorgeous. Her heart had fluttered when he said her name. That had never happened before. She turned and looked back at him, but he was moving toward the craft table. Her thoughts were racing and all jumbled. Those blue eyes...

Claire looked up at the next guy, "I'm Claire. And you are?" She could not remember his name to save her life.

"Well, I'm Mike. "His smile was wide and engaging and probably a little surprised that she didn't know his name. His handshake was a little weak, but he seemed earnest enough. She would have to work on that if he was chosen.

She smiled as he let go of her hand. Good. No electricity there.

Claire turned to Maggie, who had been watching the whole thing, and gave her a forced smile. Had she seen all of that? Could Mags see how she had reacted to the one named Andrew?

Maggie smiled at Claire. She loved when Claire met the finalists. It was fun to watch. She was usually so easy with them...smiling and laughing... and it would put them instantly at ease... until JUST NOW. Maggie kept smiling at Claire supportively, and tried to hide her surprise at the expression on Claire's face when she shook hands with the one named Andrew. Her expression was almost a blush. She would swear it. Claire had never looked like that before. She was usually all fun and business at the same time. Flirty without flirting. When she had moved on to the guy named Mike, she had even turned back to look at Andrew for a moment. This is interesting, she thought, still smiling, but for a different reason.

Chapter 8

"Can I trust you?" The text said. Maggie looked curious. Why was James texting her something so cryptic? And why was he texting her *right now*?

She was still in the "meeting" with the three finalists watching Claire work her magic with them. She wasn't sure how to answer. What did he mean by that? Trust him with what?

"Trust you with what?" She thought she would shoot straight.

"Can I trust you to help me with something that involves Claire," he typed, "and *not tell her*..." He followed quickly with, "And by asking this, I am already expecting you not to tell her about *this* conversation."

Oh, no. Maggie thought, not that. She looked straight across the room at Claire as she typed, "I

HATE KEEPING SECRETS. I'm NOT good at it" She hit send.

"I think you will like it. Please," James pleaded.

She got realistic. "Maybe you'd better run it by me before I decide. I won't tell either way."

"Okay," he relented. "Can you meet me for lunch in an hour?"

***

Maggie spotted James immediately. He was a boy version of Claire, but taller and brown eyed. She had been crushing on him since they met at Claire's birthday party two years ago, but there was no way she would admit it. He had a different pretty girl on his arm every time she saw him. She didn't want to be just another girl on his arm, so she kept it professional... always...she thought...yes, always.

"Okay, dude. What the heck. Why am I here?" She plopped down across from him at the bistro table, trying to be matter-of-fact.

"Hello to you, too, beautiful," he smiled.

She tried not to blush, but it was like trying to stop the rain. C'mon Mags, she told herself. Professional. Don't flirt back.

"Knock off the charm, James. What is going on?" She said, through clenched teeth, feigning annoyance as she put both hands flat on the table. She hoped he wouldn't see through it.

He did.

He grabbed one of her hands and brought it to his lips, and she gave in and let him kiss it. "You look great today, Maggie. Thanks for meeting me on such short notice."

She rolled her eyes, nodded, and slowly withdrew her hand. She could still feel his lips there. Dang it. She wished she could just give in and flirt back and see what would happen. He was always flirting with her. Maybe she was the girl for him... Her thoughts began to wander.

He brought her back to reality by saying, "I have a friend that I have been trying to get Claire to meet, but she keeps dodging me. I'm sure you know all about it because you are the one who reschedules each time."

Maggie nodded again, and took a sip of the water that was in front of her, "I didn't know *why* she kept rescheduling until last Friday."

"Well, this friend of mine is *perfect* for Claire, and I am being completely and totally serious. I would not send her another Karl. I hope you know that."

"I do." Maggie blushed. Immediately realizing what she had just said to him and quickly took another sip of water to hide it. "I mean, yes."

James seemed not to notice and continued, "Well, we have decided to be *proactive*."

It was the way he said "proactive" that made

her nervous all of a sudden. What was he planning?

"That sounds scary, James. Should I be nervous? Because I'm suddenly nervous."

"Uhh, maybe?" He stammered. "Now that I am saying it out loud to someone besides Andy, it's making ME nervous."

Andy? She stared at him with wide eyes. Wait a minute...Andrew?

"What have you done?" She whispered.

Chapter 9

After they had all mingled and gotten to know each other, they had all eaten the lunch provided by craft services. Claire usually included her whole production team in the selection process. The initial four-person team in charge of whittling down the mass of applicants to the final three consisted of Alice, her lighting lead, Cindy, her make-up artist, and her two psychological consultants disguised as computer nerds. Then there was Jacqui, her location scout, Sid, her lead camera operator, Missy, head of wardrobe, and Maggie, her assistant. There were 12 people in the room. Next on the schedule was when Claire explains the details of the show to the prospects to give them more to think about and to make sure they were all in, if chosen. After the details were laid out, usually one or two of them had questions and sometimes backed out. Maggie had disappeared for a while, which was not too distressing, except for the fact that she usually didn't disappear without telling anyone. Claire was impressed with all three guys and was worried now that they would have a difficult time choosing.

Maggie approached and said, "Well, boss, what do you think? Will one of them work?"

Claire nodded, "I think we will have trouble picking from these three. All of them have a spark that the camera will like, and they all have charming personalities. I'll have to compliment the team. They did good, as always. Maybe we will even use all three for the next 3 cycles. If they are willing." She paused, looking intently at Maggie, "Where did you go, by the way? No one knew where you were."

Maggie answered quickly and honestly, "I went to the bathroom." She *had* used the bathroom at the cafe.

"For an hour?" Claire raised her eyebrows. "Are you okay? Do you need to go home?"

"Uh, no, er, yes." She laughed nervously, "I mean, no, I don't need to go home, and yes, I am fine. Just a stomach thing that is settling down." That part was true. She was experiencing an intermittent nervous stomach now that she knew about "plan B."

James had explained the "plan" and asked for her help. Her help involved simply making sure that Andrew got picked for the show. How she was to accomplish that, she hadn't a clue. She had been too overwhelmed with the details of the crazy plan to remember to tell James what she had noticed about how Claire acted when she met Andrew for the first time. She would have to tell him later. She needed to think right now, and she was having a hard time thinking with Claire eyeing her with a mixture of concern and suspicion. At least she assumed that's what it was.

Her mind was whirling when Andrew approached them.

"So, ladies, what is next for today?" Andrew tilted his head back for a last sip of his soda, and then he smiled at Claire. "I'm having fun already."

"I'm glad to hear that," Claire smiled self-consciously and continued, "The next phase will include a detailed explanation of everything you should expect for the duration of the show. You will be able to make an educated decision as to whether or not you want to continue." He had been looking straight into her eyes the whole time. His eyes were smiling. Talk about active listening. She had never experienced this before. Usually, men looked all around her while she spoke to them—distracted by every little thing going on in the room. How refreshing, and yet, a little disconcerting. She met his gaze in an effort to return the compliment. It was meaningful—looking into someone's eyes like that. Connection. That was the first thing that she thought of. Connection. She felt butterflies in her stomach as his eyes continued gazing into hers. Windows to the soul...

Can you see my soul, Andrew? Her eyes questioned. His eyes softened a little and seemed to answer in the affirmative.

"Well," Claire broke the connection abruptly and looked away awkwardly, "It's time to get started. If you could take a seat over there…" She indicated the area in the room with chairs set in a circle and turned to walk in that direction. Andrew didn't move and continued to watch her as he took a long breath in. After an exhale, and with a look of determination, he made his way to the circle.

Maggie was dumbstruck. She was sure she just watched two people speak to each other without words. It had given her goosebumps. They don't need us, James, she thought. It's already happening.

Chapter 10

"So, if you are all willing to sign these waivers and legal documents, we can assume you are all-in for the duration, yes?" Claire smiled and nodded at all three of the contestants sitting in front of her. "We will be making our final selection before Friday. We will be letting you know either way. Thank you so much for your patience today."

The men stood and moved in unison to shake her hand. Drake got to her first and expressed his thanks a little too eagerly, but who could blame him. It was the last impression he would make. Andy decided to hang back and be last. He watched her as Mike shook her hand, leaned in closer and muttered something that made her laugh. Crap, Andy thought, what can I say that will keep her glowing like that? He dipped into his bag of wits and came up with a dead fish.

"I got nothing but a dead fish." He said as he

shook her hand. Deadpan.

"What?" Claire burst out laughing, shaking her head.

"I wanted to say something witty like Mike apparently did, and all I could think of was a dead fish." Andy admitted. "It's all I got for my terrific last impression."

He backed away in an exaggerated bow, and left the room.

Claire looked at Maggie, with a surprised smile. "What the...!"

"Lasting, last impression, I'd say" Maggie rolled her eyes. What a dork, she thought.

"It was memorable for sure." Claire agreed. She shook her head to herself as she took a seat in the circle with the others. I like that guy, she thought, he has an engaging personality.

"Okay, team, what do we think? Impressions?"

They spent the rest of the afternoon picking apart everything about the three men who had been on display all morning. Many of them agreed that all three were fantastic, but there were a few who had favorites. Maggie was a fan of Andrew, of course. Sid and Alice agreed that he was the most photogenic of the three. Sid had taken some pics earlier and had them to show. Her computer/head shrinks agreed that Mike and Andrew were the least phased by some of their questions during their conversations, and would probably be the most emotionally stable of the three. Alice already had ideas on how to dress Drake and Andrew, and

Cindy finally admitted that her favorite was Andrew.

I'm not going to have to be too over-persuasive here, thought Maggie. It looked to her like the room was favoring Andrew.

"Okay folks, let's sleep on it, and meet up for breakfast across the street tomorrow morning at 8. Be ready to name one favorite." Claire stood up and everyone else followed.

Maggie texted James, "We need to meet again."

Chapter 11

As Maggie pulled up to James's house, she was mentally kicking herself for getting involved in this. With a body full of imaginary bruises, she got out of the car and walked up to the door. Not only am I lying to my BOSS now, but I'm swimming in the pool of temptation with Mr. Drop-Dead-Gorgeous-Flirt-Boy. What have I done to myself?

She took a deep breath and rang the bell.

James opened immediately as if he had been waiting there at the door. She jumped. "What the...you startled me. Are you looking through the peephole or something?"

"Of course I am. I have been waiting right here since we arranged this meeting." James bowed and opened the door all the way to let her in and she noticed he wasn't alone. Andrew was standing just inside the doorway as if he had just arrived.

"Oh FAB." Maggie rolled her eyes and threw her head back and stepped through the door. "GREAT...Both conspirators. What is WRONG with you guys! Are you out of your minds? You have to be out of your stinking minds to think that you are going to be successful with this. Your own SISTER, for heaven's sake. James." She waved her arms wildly at them. All her stress from keeping this secret all day came tumbling out.

James grabbed her arms just below her shoulders and brought his head level with hers. "Maggie." He looked into her eyes with that half-flirty, half-endearing look. No. It was full-on endearing. She melted. "Maggie, please. Let's sit down over here." He led her slowly over to the sofa in the living room.

They all sat down. Maggie and James on the sofa, and Andy on the chair opposite them, and there was a significant moment of silence. Significant. Almost uncomfortable until Andy said, to no one in particular, "I knew there was something there. Just looking at her PICTURE..." He trailed off. He was clearly lost—in torment. He reached up and ran his hand through his hair. "I knew we shouldn't have done this, James. I can't go through with this. I signed every paper, but I'll just call tomorrow and back out." He slid forward on the sofa so he could stand up. "Maybe I can just call her now that she knows me and ask her out or something...you know... the normal way."

"NO." Maggie, surprised to hear herself yell

out, threw up her hands in an effort to stop him from standing. What was she doing? She heard herself continue. "I watched you today. You and Claire. Separate and together. There is a palpable chemistry between you. I know she was affected by you. She was...different than she usually is at these meets. I could feel it when you spoke to each other." She looked from James to Andy. "BUT... I firmly believe if you tried to connect with her "normally" she would not accept. No matter what she may have felt...she'll talk herself out of it... she is still too closed off to allow for the possibility."

Maggie was surprised to hear herself say all of these things, but as she said them out loud, she knew that it was all true. She could see Andrew's integrity from what he had just said. He was clearly not just thinking of himself, but of Claire's feelings as well. But Claire would have to really get to know him before she would even consider opening herself up, and the only way that was going to happen was if she was forced to. Andrew needed to be the new Single.

Chapter 12

James grabbed her hand and squeezed it. "See, Maggie, I knew you would come around to my way of thinking."

She pulled her hand away and almost slapped him in mock horror. "Don't you dare think that I'm happy about this. This is still a nightmare. This is NOT going to be easy, and I don't want to lose my best friend, much less my JOB." She moved away from him on the small sofa. Then she laughed. She couldn't escape the absurdity of what they were doing. It was too much. James and Andy looked at her, incredulous. Then she stopped laughing and started shaking her head with wide eyes. She was crazy. How could she even entertain pulling this off?

She pointed at Andy, "You better be good, buddy...and sincere... because Claire is smart and she will see right through you." She stared at him.

"And then...you're done."

"And another thing," She continued to both of them, "I was thinking of this on the way over. Have you planned on the fact that there are going to be ten...TEN other girls falling all over you every day for weeks? Girls who are perfectly matched for you? Hmmm?"

"Well..." Andy stammered, "We figured I would fake some of my answers on those computer questions, so the girls wouldn't really be my perfect match."

"Maybe James doesn't remember, or maybe he didn't know this to begin with, but Claire sits in on the entire computer interview process. It's pretty much the secret to the show's success. Claire gets to know each Single almost better than they know themselves. It is how she is able to orchestrate the dates and the situations to highlight the girls; everything about them...their character flaws, their abilities, their personalities. They may be compatible according to the computer, but you cannot substitute the day to day. The reality. Pardon the pun. If you fake your answers, you are giving those answers to her as well. You want her to know the real you, not the fake one, right?"

They sat in silence for a minute. Thinking.

James spoke first. "We need to figure out how to get her out of that room for at least a FEW minutes right? Maybe longer?"

Maggie nodded with a smirk. "Good luck with THAT. It's part of her process. It is non-negotiable.

She never misses."

"That is why we need you." James looked endearingly at Maggie and made a show of reaching for her hand again.

"Oh no...nope," Maggie shook her head and slapped her hands on her knees. "I've done all I signed up for. You boys are on your own. I will be cheering you on, but I will not be involved from this moment on."

She stood and walked to the door. When she opened the door, she turned back to them. They were both staring at her with mouths agape. "Good luck." She whispered, and was gone.

"Man. What are we going to do," Andy put his head in his hands.

After a minute, he looked up when James said softly, "I think I have an idea."

James was smiling, but he also looked like he was going to be sick.

Chapter 13

Claire set her drink down and picked up the slips of paper. Her team sat back in their chairs and waited for the verdict. They had each written their choice on a slip of paper, and now was the moment of reckoning. Claire started sorting the slips on the table. The "Andrew" pile was growing faster than the others. Maggie had mixed feelings, and didn't know how to react. She really wanted Claire to get to know Andy...*She* had voted for him, of course. But now she was torn. She didn't want to hurt Claire, but she could tell that he really liked her, and seemed like the type of guy who would do the right thing. James was the engine behind this train. Idiot James. If he wasn't so handsome and charming... Stop it.

"It looks like Andrew is our next Single!" Claire declared with a big smile. He had won by a landslide. "Maggie, get a message to him, and to the others. Let's get this party started next week. Have Andrew come in Monday at eight, and we will start the interview process and choose the girls."

Claire continued to the group, "I still have to do the edit for Cycle 12 the rest of this week, but the rest of you can start prepping for Andrew. You know your jobs. It's why we are the best crew in the city."

The crew finished their breakfast and grabbed coffees to go, and headed across the street to get to work.

Maggie grabbed both drinks and she and Claire walked together up to the editing studio. Both lost in thought. As Claire opened the studio door, she suddenly asked, "What do you think?" jarring Maggie from her thoughts.

"Hmm?" Maggie turned to her, "What do I think about what?"

"Really?...What do you think about our choice?"

"I'm sorry, my brain was somewhere else." Maggie lied, and continued quickly, "Well, I wrote Andrew's name down, so I'm happy about it.

"Good." Claire nodded. "I think he will be a fantastic Single."

Maggie took her seat in front of the monitors and smiled at Claire. She decided to ask. "What do you like about him?"

"What do I like?" Claire looked startled. It wasn't like she hadn't been asked this same question about all of the previous Singles. But this time, it seemed like a personal question instead of a professional one. It was like Maggie could see right through her. Her curiosity. Her intense attraction. She had to mentally shake that feeling and project a professional front. What would she say before? How did she used to answer this question? She couldn't remember. Good grief. I'm losing it, she thought.

"Well, he's handsome, for sure. Perfectly photogenic. Cindy said that she wouldn't need to use much make-up, and Sid and Alice agreed he would be easy for lighting and camera. I'm interested to see the girls who get matched. He may make our jobs really easy." She was rambling. Did she say stuff like this before? Could Maggie see how she was feeling? She felt absolutely transparent. She looked down and made a show of shuffling the paperwork in her lap.

It was all Maggie could do not to smile and give Claire a hard time, but she didn't dare. She could see that Claire was rattled and attempting to pull it together. She was trying to say all the right things. Maggie wanted to give Claire the chance to confide in her about how she was feeling, but she would have to wait. Maybe later an opportunity would present itself.

She decided to break the tension. "I think he is dreamy. I think I'll upload my profile to the website. His eyes were so blue; I wanted to take a swim." She had drawn her hands up and clasped them under her chin and was looking up at the ceiling. "Do you think I would be a match?"

Claire looked horrified for a minute and then relaxed and laughed when she looked up and saw Maggie's expression, "Are you nuts? Knock it off."

Bill, the editing tech walked in just then and they all got down to business making the Ann and Zack finale a masterpiece.

Chapter 14

"This will sound lame, but I need to reschedule this time, sis," James texted late Friday afternoon.

"So, you've finally given up the fight?" Claire answered. "Good."

"No, you dork, you're still going to meet my friend, but he is going to busy working on a project for the next few weeks, so he doesn't have time for you. You blew it, big time, little sis. He's a really good guy. You can't let him get away."

Claire smirked at her phone. He's clueless. I'll gladly let him get away. That was the whole point. "Yessir." She typed, and then added about 5 eye-roll emojis and hit send.

"She thinks she's off the hook," James laughed at Andy, who was in the car with him. "Little does she know…"

"You are enjoying this." Andy shook his head. "No fair. We need to get *you* interested in someone so you can see how this feels."

"Wait a minute, how do you know that I don't already know how it feels?" James started the car and pulled away from the curb. They were headed to the batting cages to hit.

"Uh-huh. Right. Nice try." Andy stared out the window. "I just can't stop thinking about her. What is she doing right now?"

James laughed, "I can *guaranTEE* you she's… wait, its Friday… so she's on her way home to heat up something in the microwave for dinner, or maybe she'll drive-thru for something. Then she'll eat it all while she watches something she's recorded on TV. Probably a romantic comedy for research. She gets ideas for her shows from movies. Another definite will be a bowl of ice-cream. Mocha almond fudge." He was drumming on the steering wheel to the music, and hit the air cymbals on "fudge." "Or maybe Haagen Dazs: coffee or strawberry."

"She's not going out somewhere?" Andy asked. "I'd love to just sit and eat and watch TV on a Friday. I'll take the Haagen Dazs coffee."

***

CRACK. Andy hit the baseball hard and high into the net on the back wall.

"That one was GONE, dude. Homerun." James stood up. It was his turn.

"Are you still seeing...what was her name? Ashley?" Andy handed the bat to James.

"Amber." James corrected him, and took his batting stance. "And, no. She moved to Atlanta. For her job, I think." The ball came whizzing toward him and he swung and missed. He smacked the bat on the plate in mock frustration. Did Andy have this on the fastball setting? Show off.

Andy laughed and sat down on the other side of the fence. "Wasn't Amber the name of your girlfriend sophomore year?"

"Yes, as a matter of fact, Mr. Know-it-all." James got ready for the next pitch. "Actually, if you must know, I have dated three girls named Amber in my young life. I've often thought that they should all be named Amber so that I don't accidently call one of them the wrong name."

"It's the law of averages, my *old* playboy friend." Andy said knowingly. "You are getting up there. You need to start looking for the right girl. Unless you are planning on being single your whole life."

"Excuse me, friend," James took his final swing and missed again. "I *am* looking. Why do you think I go on so many dates with different women? I haven't found one who I connect with, yet."

Andy entered the cage to take his turn and they switched places again. James slumped onto the bench. Andy hit ball #1, and then ball #2. James stood up and clapped. "You are on fire, dude!"

Andy smiled and continued to hit ball after ball.

They didn't bother switching. Andy was always more athletic than James. James didn't care. He wasn't one of those macho dudes who had to one-up everyone. He was happy with his life. At least he thought he was until his best friend had started asking about Claire. And since Andy had met her earlier this week, he was different. More focused. More serious about life. That is what James didn't have. The focus. The future outlook. The goals. That's it.

"You know, Andy, I've noticed that you have changed just a little in this last week."

"Good or bad?"

"Well, I think you are more focused on the future. I have been trying to put my finger on it. I think you have become more goal oriented. You have a plan."

"You thought of the plan, doofus."

"No, no, not *that* plan. I'm serious." James tried to explain. "You don't talk about the little things. You are quieter. Like you are thinking more." He paused. "I want that."

"It's all about the girl." Andy smiled.

Chapter 15

"Okay, I'll come clean," James said suddenly and out-of-the-blue. They were back at James' house stuffing themselves full of pizza, again.

"Uh…What?" Andy said, surprised. "Come clean? Are you dirty? What do you mean? Are you hiding something?" He laughed out loud.

"Kind-of," James admitted seriously. "You keep saying I need to find a girl, and I start to argue, but you drop it way too easily, like you don't believe me."

Andy stared. "Wait a minute, now. Do you have a certain girl already in mind?" He put his pizza down and sat forward in the chair. "Come on. You've got me now. Spill."

"It's probably nothing because she doesn't give me the time of day. Well, that's not true, really. She knows me, and talks to me, but she doesn't flirt with me, so that makes me think that she isn't interested. I'm used to girls flirting back and melting at my every word. This one doesn't do that."

"Are you sure you aren't just interested because she *isn't*?"

"I don't think so. I've thought about that. I have. I've known her for a few years, now, and I just like so many things about her. She is gorgeous, but doesn't know it. I consider her a good friend, and I can be myself around her. She makes that part easy because she doesn't respond to my advances, so I've had to back off a little and just be friends, and I like it. There's no pressure." He was excited to finally say it out loud to someone besides the mirror.

Andy could tell James had feelings for this girl. "Do I know her?" He had his suspicions. He had only witnessed one girl rebuff James, and it was within the last week.

"I don't know if I should say."

"It's Maggie." Andy said it for him, "Right?"

"Are you *kidding*?" James was shocked. "Are you *psychic*?"

"It's got to be Maggie. She is the only "friends-only" girl in your life that I know of. And didn't you meet her about 2 years ago?"

Andy continued. "Do you only see her when Claire is there? At family events? Events where you take dates? You know, if the only time she sees you, you are with a different girl…." He tapped his temple with his forefinger. "Did you ever think that your overly active dating behavior may be the reason why she stays clear of you? I would if I were a girl." Andy got up to get another soda from the kitchen.

Woah. Good point, Andy, James thought. I hadn't considered that. She could just be protecting herself.

"What should I do?" James asked.

Andy laughed again, "What? Now you want advice from me? Funny."

"No really, Andy. What do you think?"

"If it were me, I'd make sure she sees me *without* another girl for a *large* span of time."

"Done," James nodded. "I'm ready."

"But are you ready for *Monday*?" Andy looked at him with concern. "I can't believe you are actually going to do this."

James grimaced and nodded. "I'm ready if you are. Make it count. Don't make me suffer for nothing."

Chapter 16

"Andrew, this is Ethan and Marcus. They work the computer magic to find your true love." Claire introduced Andy to the two men sitting at the two computers in the small room next to the one where he met Claire last week. Andy shook hands with both of them across the table and then sat down on one of the other two chairs in the room. The computers and their nerds sat on one side of an oblong table and the two other chairs that held Claire and Andy were on the opposite side. Andy could see their faces partially and guessed that they would be buried in the screens for the most part and not focused on him. Good, he hoped.

"Would you like a water?" Ethan asked Andy, and indicated a little fridge next to the cabinets on one of the walls. "There's water in there, if you want, and candy and snacks over there." He pointed to a shelf across from the door. "Help yourself. This is a long process, but we try to make it just a little bit fun." Andy looked around at the room. It was painted a blue denim color and had some beach scene art and a large painting of what looked like the Getty in Malibu on one wall, and a small window on the other that was shaded with a blue and white polka dot fabric curtain. Blue walls, he laughed to himself. Boy, my eyes be poppin' today.

Andy looked at Claire. She was tapping on her phone and she had a notebook in her lap. Her hair was pushed behind her ears and she was biting her lower lip in concentration. She was irresistible. He watched her as long as he could without looking creepy to the two other guys. They were too busy focused on their computers to notice, but still. He didn't want to blow this on the first day. He was just a bit nervous. He planned to be completely honest with his answers unless Claire wasn't in the room. He wasn't sure how long she would be gone, if James' plan worked at all. If it didn't work, and she didn't leave, that would make her pretty callous and cold, and both he and James agreed she wasn't callous and cold. So, he would keep his eyes on the clock. The magic hour was supposed to be sometime around 10.

They started with basic questions about his childhood. Dates. Places. People. How did he feel about his childhood? Did he have a pet growing up? Did he have one now? Some of the questions were bizarre. His favorite was the one about what his least favorite song was when he was 16. The question was so weirdly specific. It took him less than 5 seconds to think of it, though. "'Oops, I Did it Again.' Hands down."

Claire sat unobtrusively back from the table and slightly behind him, so he couldn't look at her unless he turned around and made it obvious. He would try to rectify that after a break—angle his chair differently somehow, or maybe sit in hers. She rarely spoke, but she was taking notes. He just tried to be as sincere as he could. James told him he was afraid he wouldn't be a good enough actor. This wasn't acting. He was legitimately nervous and legitimately trying to tell them everything; which was the same as telling her everything. If she didn't like what she heard, there was no reason to go further. He wanted her to know him completely and honestly even though the whole process was based on pretense. This was patently ridiculous. She would know all about him, and he would know almost nothing about her. Maybe he could sneak in some questions for her now and then. He wanted to know everything.

He had returned from a stretching break around 9:30, when Claire's phone buzzed. "Oh no," She looked at the screen startled and concerned. "Excuse me for a minute. Just hang tight."

Andy looked at Ethan and Marcus as she left the room, and they looked back at him with surprise and concern. "This happen often?" He asked.

"Uh, no." Marcus offered. "She never leaves the room, normally."

"Should we keep going?" Andy asked quickly, knowing what the message had been, and not knowing how much time he had.

Marcus and Ethan looked at each other sideways and Ethan said a quick, "No."

Marcus continued, "She never misses a question. It is part of the process. We can't go on without her. She said she'd just be a minute. Just relax."

Silence took over. It would have been easy to relax, because the chairs were surprisingly comfortable, but at that moment, he was just a tad below terrified on the fright scale. Then all three of them heard Claire's voice through the door, "OHMYGOSH, IS HE OKAY?" She must have been standing right outside the door.

Then Maggie's voice, also on the edge of hysterical, started out faint and got louder as if she was running down the hall toward Claire, "I don't know, the hospital just said he was in stable condition. I don't know if that is okay, or if he is really bad. Or maybe they said critical condition. I don't remember now. I freaked out. I'm sorry, Claire."

The three men looked at each other with obvious concern. Critical condition? Andy thought, good gravy, James, you were just supposed to crash on your bicycle on the way to work. Maybe break an arm. What did you do? He felt sick to his stomach.

The door opened and Claire walked in with Maggie. She was visibly upset. There were tears in her eyes and she was shaking. She looked frantically at Ethan and Marcus. "My brother... has been in an accident. I have to go."

"Do you want us to hold? Do you want pick it up again tomorrow?" Ethan asked.

"Uhh...I don't..." Claire was trying to put together a coherent thought, "...know. Guys, do you think you could finish Day One without me? I don't know how bad it is. I may be back in an hour... I don't know. I just know that I told the network we would be ready for an initial promo shoot Tuesday of next week, so we need to..."

"Got it, boss." Marcus was all business trying to be a steady voice for her. "We can go over today's stuff with you later. Get out of here. Your brother needs you."

Claire put her hand on Andrew's shoulder and looked at him through her tear-filled eyes and apologized sincerely, and added something about him being in good hands. She turned and left the room. Maggie also looked at him, but her expression, although frantic, was markedly different. Daggers. Were those daggers flying from her eyes? She looked like she was going to say something, but he implored her with his eyes to stay silent. Somehow, he was able to communicate that he was just as concerned as she was. Her eyes softened. She turned and left.

"So, Andrew, how many girlfriends did you have in high school?"

Chapter 17

Claire and Maggie ran through the doors into the hospital. It had taken 20 minutes longer than it was supposed to according to the traffic App, but that was L.A. for you. At least it wasn't raining; no one in L.A. knew how to drive in the rain. You never knew how long it was going to take to get anywhere at any time of day anymore. They were both frantic. The call Maggie had received from the studio receptionist had just said that James was at Community General, he had been in an accident involving his bicycle and a bus; he was in stable condition and was asking for his sister.

Claire ran right at the receptionist, "Excuse me! I got a call that my brother was in an accident. James Culver. Where is he, please?"

The receptionist smiled compassionately and looked at her screen. "Third floor. Take the second bank of elevators. Bed 3115."

As they got to the elevators, Maggie felt her phone vibrate, but was too concerned about James to care. The elevator seemed to take forever. Only three floors. It felt like 30.

When they found the room with bed 3115, they held onto each other for support as they walked through the door.

Both women stopped still, "Ohmygosh!" they both said in unison.

James was propped up in bed, his left leg was elevated on a pillow, and in a cast, his left arm was in a sling, he had bandages on his cheeks and forehead, and he appeared to be sleeping.

"James." Claire took 3 steps to his left side and touched his shoulder, careful not to touch any part of him that might hurt. He didn't open his eyes. "James, honey, it's me. It's Claire. I'm here now. You are going to be fine." She leaned over and kissed the part of his forehead that wasn't covered in a bandage.

There was only one bed in the room, so Maggie went around the long way to the right side of the bed and gingerly covered his right hand with hers. She didn't know what to say. She was mad. Her guess was that he had done this on purpose to get Claire out of the interview with Andy. He looked so broken. A part of her was proud that he would make this crazy sacrifice for his friend and, ultimately, his sister, but she was mostly mad. She sat down in the chair next to the bed.

Claire straightened his blanket, absently fixed

things on his hospital gown, and carefully brushed his hair with her fingers, but she was antsy. She was impatient to find out all the details. After about a minute she declared, "I am going to find the doctor, or someone who knows what's going on." Maggie nodded at her and Claire left the room. Maggie looked back at James and he opened his right eye, and turned his right hand so he could hold hers to keep her there.

"Is she gone?"

Despite her instinct to pull her hand away, Maggie let him hold her hand. He had a tight grip. She didn't want to hurt him. "You're awake? How come you didn't say anything to Claire? She is frantic. What the heck happened? Are you okay?"

"Did you get my text?"

"No. When did you send it?

"About 5 minutes ago, just before you walked in," He lifted the arm that was in the sling. It was obviously not injured and was hiding his phone. "I didn't want you to worry, so I tried to warn you." He smiled humbly into her eyes. He moved his phone onto the side table.

She took out her phone and read the text, "I'm not hurt badly but don't tell Claire that." She made a face. "Nice brother. Now I'm grateful I don't have a brother."

"No really, Maggie. It's true. I broke my leg, but that's it. I talked the nurse into this sling and these bandages, and the story about the bus. I'm trying to buy time for Andy. The more I'm hurt, maybe the longer she'll stay?" He was still holding tight to her hand.

"You idiot. You had me so scared that you had done something stupid and dangerous." She paused. "But this was still stupid. And dangerous. How bad is your leg?"

"It's just a hairline shin fracture. I jumped off my roof." He made a face. "I was hoping to just break an ankle, but I landed too far forward. It hurt so bad I couldn't take a breath at first. I waited until Mr. Martinez across the street was taking his trash cans to the curb, so he would hear me yell and bring me to the hospital. I had the ladder out so he wouldn't question my fall."

"How did you talk the nurse into all these lies...and supplies?"

"I told her that I was trying to garner sympathy from a lovely lady?" He batted his eyelashes at her.

"No really," She wasn't having it, "how did you do it?"

He hadn't wanted to tell her this, but it was better to be honest. And he was turning over a new leaf with Maggie. Here goes. "Well, if you must know, one of the nurses that works here...well...was a girl I dated for a bit a few years ago." There. He said it. He quickly added, "But not anymore."

"And she was willing to do all this for what? Another date?" Maggie was not sure why she asked this. It sounded like she cared too much.

"I guess just to be helpful and in on a secret

with me." James sighed. "I took advantage of an old friendship, and I probably shouldn't have. I *did* tell her that I was seeing someone else so that she didn't get any ideas."

"Are you?"

"Am I what?" James knew exactly what, but he wanted her to say it.

"Seeing someone else?" She tried not to blush, and suppressed the urge to pull her hand away. His hand was warm and soft. He had loosened his grip a little, and she was loving the feeling of his hand gently in hers.

He could see she was rattled just a teeny bit, and hoped she wouldn't bolt out of the room. Play it cool, James, he thought. Don't scare her off.

"No." he said casually. "I don't think I've been on a date for at least 3 weeks. I've been so consumed with Andy's love life that I've let myself go."

Really, Maggie thought. Interesting. She didn't think she remembered a time when he had not had a girlfriend or at least a girl he was dating. "I don't know if I believe that." She moved her hand a little, and he immediately held on a little tighter. She let herself look down at her hand and then back at him.

"Maggie, really?" He said in earnest. "You don't believe me?"

"Um, of course I believe you," she said sarcastically. "Because you are never without a girl on your arm." There. She said it out loud. To him.

"It is kind-of embarrassing, if I'm honest. I mean...not for me... but for you...you know...to have that kind of reputation. Just sayin'."

He took it well. Like he was expecting it. She was impressed. He looked thoughtful and sad. She could only hope that he wasn't acting.

"I'm sorry." He squeezed her hand. "You are the last person I want to have a negative image of me..."

Suddenly Claire could be heard outside the door, "I am NOT kidding. Someone better have some answers for me about my brother."

Dang it, Maggie thought. James was just starting to...

Claire walked in, frantic. "I can't find a single soul who will answer my questions."

Maggie watched Claire walk back in and James squeezed her hand. She looked back at James and his eyes were closed like he was when they had first walked in. He squeezed her hand again, and she squeezed back as if to say, "Yes, Dumb-Dumb, I'll keep your secret." She didn't want to admit to Claire that she had been having a conversation with James, because she would just demand the details and Maggie wanted to avoid those details. All of them. The Andy detail, *and* the I-like-your-brother detail.

Maggie shrugged at Claire and tried to look concerned. She wasn't sure if she was succeeding when suddenly Claire gasped, "James! James! Honey, are you okay? What happened?"

James had opened his eyes groggily and was looking at Claire with a confused expression. "Where...where am I?" James made his voice sound gravelly. Maggie closed her eyes to suppress the urge to roll her eyes. Now he was definitely acting.

"You are in the hospital, buddy." Claire sat down on his left side. "Do you remember what happened?"

He closed his eyes and looked thoughtful. "Oh yeah. It's all coming back. I was on my bike. There was a bus. I swerved to avoid it and crashed into a tree. My arm is really hurting, could you get some Tylenol for me?"

She jumped up and said, "Of course buddy, I'll be right back." She practically ran out of the room to find a nurse.

"It's all coming back." Maggie mimicked him. "Brilliant performance."

He smiled proudly and brought her hand up to his lips and gave it a long, lingering kiss without breaking eye contact while the butterflies in her stomach did jumping jacks. "Thank you, my dear."

Chapter 18

Andy was actually having fun being a total cad. Well, his version of it anyway. They were asking all about high school and college, and even though he was not a big ladies' man for that 8-year period, he tried to make like he was. He was wracking his brain about how to answer the questions to match girls that he would not be attracted to. He was not a psychologist, but his mom told him once to be the person that you want to attract. So, he was doing the opposite. It was all he could do not to laugh at some of his answers. He was trying to be genuine as well. And he thought that some questions deserved honesty. What if Claire looked at these closely? He wanted at least some of them to be real.

He couldn't have known that both Marcus and Ethan were licensed psychologists and experts in human behavior. Only Claire knew that. She didn't want that to become public knowledge, so she was the only one who knew. Their HR files said nothing of their psych degrees. Only computer skills. If only Maggie had known this...

"So, you are saying that you enjoy surfing?" Ethan asked again.

"Oh yeah, dude. Surfing is totally awesome." Andy adopted his best surfer accent to make them laugh, "When I'm in the tube, its super knarly, and I'm totally stoked. Best feeling ever." He threw up his hand in a hang loose gesture. "No really." He said in his normal voice, "I don't do much surfing anymore, but in high school I was at the Wedge in Newport most days every summer.

Ethan gave Marcus a look and kept going. "Do you still have a board?"

"I think my mom had my board in her garage until they moved back east." He looked thoughtful. "I don't know if they took it with them...probably not." He was regretting this line of questioning. The thought just occurred to him that Claire might choose to plan a surfing activity since there were beaches everywhere you looked in Southern California. He had never surfed before. He was getting carried away. He needed some air.

"Hey, guys, can I take a restroom break?" Andy asked. He had been sucking back the water so he could ask this very question whenever he needed to.

Both men nodded and Andy left the room.

"You get the same feeling I'm getting?" Marcus

spoke first.

Ethan nodded, "If it's the feeling that this nut has Multiple Personality Disorder, then YES."

Marcus laughed. "Well, maybe not that drastic. I keep getting the feeling that he's not sure what to say, but wants to make a certain impression. Maybe he is just nervous. This *is* an uncomfortable process. I wouldn't want to answer all these questions."

"I'm just glad Claire isn't here. She would kick him to the curb." Ethan put his hands on top of his head. "One of the first things he told us was about being deathly afraid of sharks as a child. Now he's a professional surfer?" He threw up his hands.

"Well, he was more at ease with Claire here," Marcus admitted. "Maybe we should take an early lunch and hope she gets back by then."

When Andy returned, Marcus made up an excuse about the software glitching and told him to take an early lunch and to be back at 1. Andy said "okay" and left again.

He didn't know whether to be grateful or worried. Were they seeing right through him? They had done this for 12 other guys already. He had no idea how the others did. Oh well, he thought as he left the building, I got at least two and a half hours of crazy in there. Claire had said this process lasted 2 full days, so there was still time for him to show her the real him.

Chapter 19

"You have to stop doing that." Maggie said very softly. James was still holding her hand to his lips. There was no way she was going to move, so those words seemed silly even as she said them.

"But I like it." He said just as softly. "Please don't say I can't kiss you, Maggie."

The butterflies in her stomach were going crazy. She was frozen in place; locked in a staring contest with the most handsome man on the planet. Even with all the bandages, he was hands down the most beautiful thing she had ever seen; even more so when he looked at her like that, and said her name. She liked how her name sounded when he said it.

He lowered her hand just as Claire ran back in the room ahead of a nurse who was carrying a plastic cup with medicine and a cup of water with a straw. The nurse was young and perky and had on a little more make-up that you would have thought was appropriate for a nurse. Her name tag said, "Amber." Didn't Claire say that James' most recent girlfriend was named Amber? But he just said that the nurse friend was from a few *years* ago. She slowly pulled her hand away from his. I don't believe this, she thought. Her heart stopped talking and her head took over.

He reached out to take the medicine cup from Amber and thanked her. She winked at him so that only he and Maggie could see, and left the room.

He downed the pills and rested his head against the pillow. Maggie could tell he was in pain, but he was trying to do two things at once. Make a brave face for her and a broken face for Claire. It was almost comical. She could see both, but fortunately Claire could only see the broken one. She half listened to Claire go on and on about James being more careful. She was rambling, and it was easy for Maggie to let her mind whirl into a frenzy over this Amber person who had just helped James, and winked at James, and was probably wearing too much make-up specifically for James. Was he being honest? Was he playing her? She had gone from butterflies and bliss, to dismay in about 10 seconds.

I'm such an idiot, she thought as she excused herself to use the bathroom. She could feel James' eyes on her as she walked out of the room.

She had to find out. She wasn't the best personal assistant in the industry for nothing. She marched over to the nurses' station as she quickly thought of a line of questioning. Another nurse was sitting there. "Do you know where the nurse named Amber is?" Maggie asked sweetly. "She just brought the patient in 3115 some meds."

The nurse looked up at Maggie and squinted, "There was a nurse named Amber here just a bit ago, but she isn't assigned to this floor normally, so I don't know her. I think she is a floater today. She mentioned she usually works in Emergency, but took a floating shift today for extra hours."

"Oh," Maggie used her most disappointed face, "I was hoping to ask her a few questions about my friend's condition. She seemed to be familiar with his situation. Is she still around?"

The nurse looked up at a schedule on the wall and shook her head. "It looks like she just floated." She paused and then laughed. "I'm sorry; I guess that might sound funny."

Maggie put her hand to her forehead in frustration and turned to leave.

"Wait. I think she said she was on her way to the NICU."

"Where is that, please?" Maggie looked relieved.

Chapter 20

As Maggie rounded the corner on the fifth floor, she spotted Amber immediately. She was standing by the nurses' station holding a clipboard and looking up at the wall schedule.

As she got closer, she noticed Amber's make-up was all but gone. Maggie summoned her sweetest smile from deep down, because she certainly wasn't feeling it. "Um. Hi." She waved shyly at Amber, "Weren't you the nurse that brought my friend, James, his meds just a minute ago? The nurse downstairs said I could find you here. I hope you don't mind."

Amber looked embarrassed and not sure what to say. "Why, yes. That was me, of course. Does he need anything?" She was visibly confused and flustered. Maggie assumed it was because she was the one who had lied about his condition to the studio receptionist and didn't know how far to take it, now.

"No. He is okay for now. Thank you." Maggie tried to put her at ease. "His sister and I were just wondering how bad his arm and leg are. We haven't been able to locate his doctor."

"You're not his sister?" Amber asked. "You are his friend, right?"

Maggie nodded and Amber lowered her voice and eyed Maggie knowingly, "Oh good. He told me specifically not to talk to his sister. Just his friends. He said there would probably be a girl and a guy. You are the girl, right?"

Maggie almost laughed out loud. "Yes, I'm the girl." This was hilarious. This poor thing was acting like she was in a spy movie. She was sweet, but in a battle of wits, she would be woefully unarmed. Ah James.

"I don't want to spoil his plan." She looked at Maggie innocently. "But if you're not his sister, then I can tell you. He just broke his leg. I've been with him since he showed up in Emergency, and helped cast it in Ortho before I brought him up to the room. He made me get those bandages and arm sling, and he put them on himself. I'm sorry about the lie on the phone. That wasn't you, was it? I didn't want to do that… He assured me it was for a good thing. He's hard to say 'no' to."

Oh, you better believe it, Maggie smiled. "No, that wasn't me on the phone. That was the studio receptionist."

"Oh yeah, I remember now, his sister works for

TV. That dating show, right?"

Maggie ignored the question and asked one of her own. "How do you know James? Are you two dating? I mean you would have to be close to do something this crazy for someone." She smiled disarmingly.

Amber blushed and laughed, "Oh wow, uh, no...not for a while anyway. Years. I wish..." She was clearly embarrassed. "I mean, you know...I was surprised when he called me to help him, and I thought...well...you know." She rambled. "He told me he was in a serious relationship, but that he needed...me.... for this...'cause I work here...Is he really seeing...? No wait, it's really none of my business."

Maggie decided to be honest. "I'm his sister's best friend, so I don't know that much about his personal life. I just wondered why you were willing to do this. I mean, couldn't you get in trouble?"

"Oh." She looked around. "Uh, not really. James said he would take all the responsibility if his sister freaked out." She looked nervously at Maggie. "Did she freak out?"

Maggie smiled reassuringly, "No." Then added, "Not yet, anyway."

Another nurse came into view and Amber mumbled that she had to get to work and walked away, leaving Maggie process all of it. So, he was telling her the truth after all. She slowly made her way back to the elevator. She tried to summon the warm feelings she had felt when he was holding her hand. It was harder than she thought. Her heart had gone into hiding again.

When she got off the elevator, she noticed a man standing just outside James' room. As she got closer, she recognized Andy. Was he kidding? Did he want to run into Claire? "Pssst." She tried to get his attention quietly.

Andy turned at the noise to see Maggie motioning for him to follow her, and they hurried down the hall and ducked into an empty room.

"What the *heck* are you doing here?" Maggie attacked him. Her pent-up anger at James was finding an outlet with poor Andy.

"You are not the only one who is worried about James." He countered. "At least you have been here and know what's going on, and how he is. I have been in the dark, here, for the last three hours."

"Well, for heaven's sake, don't blow it by letting Claire see you, or James will have broken his leg for nothing."

"He *broke* his leg?" Andy put his head in his hands. "What an idiot. He told me he was going to crash his bike and sprain something and just make it look worse than it actually was."

"He has an actual hairline shin fracture, and then he has fabricated some sort of arm or shoulder injury, and a bunch of facial injuries. He managed to enlist the help of a former girlfriend named Amber who works here."

"Amber?" he laughed. "Is she the one from,

like, 2 years ago that he only went out with twice?"

Maggie shrugged.

"Cause the most recent Amber moved to Atlanta over a month ago."

"How many Ambers are there?" Maggie had to laugh after all. She couldn't help it. The thought of more than two Ambers...

"Actually, Maggie, He's all talk." Andy thought he'd repay the favor James had just so generously performed for him. "James doesn't date as much as you might think. He goes on dates, but discovers pretty quickly whether or not he is interested enough to keep dating any specific girl. He's picky."

Maggie's phone buzzed. She picked it out of her pocket and unlocked the screen. It was a text from Claire. "Where are u? Are u okay? I thought u had to use restroom? Did u get lost? Lol"

Before she could think of a coherent reply, the phone buzzed again. It was from James. "Come back to me, please. Claire just left. I need to talk to you."

She looked up at Andy and before she could inform him that Claire was leaving, the phone buzzed yet again. "Good grief, people." She said to the phone. "Keep your pants on."

It was a second text from Claire, "I have to get back to studio by 1, James seems OK, wants to sleep. I'll come back after work. Meet me at car in 10."

She looked back up at Andy. "Claire just left.

We can go see him now."

Chapter 21

"Maggie, Amber is not my girlfriend." James blurted out as soon as she walked through the door.

She was taken aback, not expecting such a declaration, especially with Andy right behind her. "What? Why would I ..." She paused, then looked seriously into his eyes and added, "James, your love life is certainly none of my business."

"I wanted you to know, because you seemed bothered when you found out that the nurse that helped me was named 'Amber.'"

Perceptive, and smart, thought Maggie. A dangerous combination. She replied with a shrug, "What are you talking about?"

"You pulled your hand away."

"You had to take your medication, and I had to use the bathroom."

His brown eyes were locked on hers. He was

not going to win this, but she didn't want to get further into it with Andy standing there awkwardly. Plus, she didn't have time. Claire was probably already at the car. "I have to go."

"Please come back later?" James looked desperate. Good.

"Maybe," She turned and nodded to Andy, "He's all yours. But you probably can't stay long. See you back at the studio." She hurried out of the room and didn't smile to herself until she got in the elevator. The feeling was real. He was being honest. And the best part was he was trying as hard as he could to make sure she knew it. She wasn't sure why, but she was at least a little bit open to finding out.

***

"What was that all about?" Andy sat down in the chair Claire had recently vacated.

"I was being charming, and flirting, and she was *responding*." James said while he took his arm out of the sling, and started taking the bandages off his face, "I mean, we had a *moment* while Claire was running around trying to find the doctor. She has never looked at me quite like that before. And then *Amber* walked in looking all made up, and acting all cozy with me. Maggie got real cold, real fast. I had to set her straight."

"Do you think she believes you?" Andy looked at his watch. "I can't stay. I'm due back for The Inquisition Part II at 1." He laughed. "This is brutal, dude. You cannot imagine the questions they are asking me."

James laughed. He had removed all the bandages and was adjusting his position on the bed when he must have moved wrong and aggravated his leg break. "AAARGH." The pain interrupted his amusement at Andy's situation.

"I'm sorry, man." Andy shook his head. "I still can't believe you did this to yourself on purpose, for me. How long are you in here?"

"No worries." James held up his fist, and Andy tapped it with his fist in a fist bump. "I'll call in the favor sometime soon. They said I could go home anytime. Amber just found me this open bed for effect. She talked her friend at the reception desk into helping direct Claire here when she arrived. Can you grab the crutches that are in the closet?"

Andy grabbed the crutches as James maneuvered himself to a standing position. He grimaced as the different position affected the feeling in his broken leg. "The break isn't too bad. The doctor said I could probably change casts to a more lightweight material in two weeks, and be totally healed in less than five."

"That's good news." Andy handed him the crutches and they started moving out of the room and down the hall toward the elevators. "Do you need me to take you home?"

"Actually, yes. If you can." James admitted. "I had arranged for Amber to take me, but I don't think I want to chance that. I don't want Amber to get the wrong idea, and I certainly don't want

Maggie to somehow find out. I'll text her when we get in the car."

"It is literally the least I can do." Andy said as he punched the elevator button.

Chapter 22

As Claire and Maggie walked into the studio, they were both lost in thought, but about different things. They had discussed James' condition briefly in the car, but Claire was unable to agree with Maggie that it wasn't as bad as she thought. Maggie had tried to be positive and offered reassurance that she thought James would be okay, but Claire could not shake the fact that she had been unable to talk to a doctor about his injuries and prognosis. That was just odd. She had to take the word of a brother who was prone to downplay everything in order to protect her. The big brother in him couldn't help it. For heck's sake she was a grown woman. She could handle stuff. She had considered calling their mother, who was on a trip, but James had talked her out of it.

She had to shake the what-ifs, or she wouldn't be able to concentrate on the rest of the afternoon with Andrew. She needed her wits about her for that. Ethan had intimated that there was something up with the guy. Marcus thought it may be nerves. Well, she would see soon enough.

Maggie, on the other hand, had more positive thoughts running through her head. So, James hadn't had a date in weeks, Amber was a non-issue, and Andy had flat out said James was not the ladies' man she had always believed. She didn't know Andy very well, but she had already concluded that he was serious about getting to know Claire. That made him at least somewhat intelligent in her book. James thought he was good enough for his sister. Good enough to hurt himself on purpose. She had trouble with whether or not that was good. But it spoke to her that Andy was drawn to Claire. Someone needed to be. Claire was a great person. She was talented, and kind, and smart. Someone needed to recognize that. It appeared that Andy did, so she gave him the benefit of the doubt. She had a fleeting thought that it would be a tad romantic to have a guy do something like that in order to meet *her*. A fleeting thought.

"Would you like to sit in on the interview?" Claire interrupted Maggie's thoughts. "I have been promising to let you be more involved. It's up to you. Do you have a full day?"

Maggie smiled and thought that her day could not be going any better. "I am pretty light today. Your schedule is already set for a week. I'm good.

I'd love to."

"I'll warn you; the guys are worried that Andrew is too nervous, and is answering questions weird."

"Maybe my presence will help?" Maggie offered. Wait, she told herself. That probably didn't sound so good. She was supposed to be a stranger to him.

"Maybe," Claire agreed. "We'll know soon enough."

They got off the elevator and turned down the hall toward the interview studio. Andy was standing in the hall outside the studio finishing off a burrito. How did he get here so fast? Maggie wondered. She and Claire had stopped to get a sandwich for lunch, but she didn't think they had taken that long. She couldn't have known that he had even taken James home first.

Andy was congratulating himself on beating them to the studio as he finished the last bites of the burrito he had grabbed from the food truck in the parking lot. That was fortuitous. A lucky burrito. Let's hope the luck sticks with me, he thought, and I can start to get to know Claire.

"Hello, Andrew," Claire smiled, "I hope you are ready for more questions?" She said this so reassuringly that he forgot he was nervous. Just her voice was calming and easy. It made him feel at home.

He must have said something without realizing it or nodded because she replied, "Great to hear."

She continued with, "I hope you don't mind, but I've invited my assistant, Maggie, to join us for the rest of the afternoon. You remember Maggie?"

Maggie nodded a greeting and he said, "Of course I do. Good to see you, Maggie. By all means; the more the merrier. I hope your brother is okay?"

"Yes." She replied absently, "He says he is…"

Andy nodded and opened the door for the women and they all entered the room.

Chapter 23

Maggie was liking Andy more and more as the afternoon wore on. This interview process was hands down the best way for Claire to see who he really is. And if she didn't come away with at least a slight interest beyond professional, Maggie would eat her shirt. There was a clear attraction between them. Maggie saw it, and hoped that Ethan and Marcus would be oblivious. He was charming and clearly unaware of his attractiveness. He looked you in the eye when he spoke to you. At least he was looking Claire in the eye. The techs would ask the questions while buried in their screens, only occasionally looking up at their victim, and Andy would answer looking straight at Claire. They had covered basics of his life up until present day. He was shy in high school, was in the tech club, and played football. He had recently moved back to LA after working in Manhattan for an investment firm that had recruited him right after graduating UCLA(where he had met James). Maggie assumed the roommate he called "Jimmy" was James. There were a few hairy minutes there where Maggie thought he might slip, or at least share a story that Claire would recognize as part of James' college experience, but Claire appeared completely oblivious. Maggie wondered how she was not connecting the dots. Both men were the same age, and had attended during the same years. She never even offered up the information that her brother had attended at the same time, or the fact that she, herself, had graduated UCLA film school a few years after James. The typical, "did you know so-and-so?" question never came up. Either she just figured that it was a huge school and what were the odds, or she wanted to keep her personal life out of the process. Claire was being totally professional apart from an occasional look at Andy that lingered a little too long, and only when he wasn't looking. Maggie could only conclude that this was how Claire did every interview, and since this was Maggie's first, she had no reference.

"These next few questions are basic likes and dislikes, and then we will break until tomorrow." Marcus said with a smile. "What is your favorite fast food, and real food?"

"Let's see. Fast food would be In-n-Out, or shrimp fried rice. And real food would be steak and mashed potatoes, or sweet potato fries." Andy looked right at Claire an added, "And coffee ice-cream, preferably Haagen Dazs."

Claire's eyes widened. You've got to be kidding, she thought. She tried not to blurt out that those were her favorites as well. She was having a really hard time doing that for almost every question he answered. She had wanted to have a conversation with each one. She was enthralled with the fact that she had so much in common with this guy. She had bitten a hole in her tongue from trying to keep her mouth shut. He had even gone to the same university as her and James.

"Do you have any dislikes, when it comes to food?"

"Sushi." Andy said quickly. "That's pretty much it. I will eat just about anything, but raw fish is just not palatable.... Fully aware that this makes me an oddball in Southern California"

"Not really. I can't stand sushi, either." Claire mumbled, then looked up surprised and said, "Did I just say that out loud?" Ethan and Marcus stopped clicking and looked over the monitors at her with surprised looks.

Maggie's assumptions were correct. Claire didn't speak during these things. The looks Ethan and Marcus were giving Claire made that clear.

"I'm so sorry." Claire put her hand up to her mouth. "I'm usually quiet as a mouse during the interviews." She looked back down at her notebook and waved her hand to continue.

Andy took a chance, "I thought I was the only one in the Southland who didn't like sushi."

Claire looked up and laughed. "Me too." She leaned toward him, put her hand on his knee like an old friend and whispered, "I have prohibited craft services from providing it on set, so you don't have to worry."

Andy thought quickly and decided it was okay. He placed his hand on top of hers and said, "Thank you so much." Her touch was giving him goosebumps. Her hand was cool, but was warming his knee somehow. He removed his hand after a few seconds so it didn't seem awkward, but he would have loved to keep it there if only to warm her hand.

She removed her hand at the same time and was trying to calm the butterflies she felt when he touched her hand. His hand was warm and soft. She suppressed the urge to continue the conversation.

This exchange was not lost on Maggie. She had seen definite fireworks. But she was also watching Ethan and Marcus. They were behaving a little differently than she would have thought. They were more animated than she had seen them all afternoon; looking up at Claire, and looking at each other, and furiously typing at the same time. She would have thought they would have been bored with this, but they were more interested in this exchange than they had been in any of Andy's other answers.

Andy was electrified. He had gotten her to engage in conversation. He had started to lose hope that she was going to remain silent the whole time. He was going to keep at it. He now had hope.

Chapter 24

"He is a really great guy," Maggie began as she and Claire sat down back in Claire's office. "I really like him. Like I said before, I think I should create a profile and apply."

"Don't you dare!" Claire snapped, and then softened when she saw Maggie's expression. "Quit saying that. Why do you keep saying that?"

"Do you like him?" Maggie asked. She was fishing. She wondered how she could let Claire know it was okay to share her feelings. Maybe if Claire knew that Maggie had noticed her looking at him when she thought no one would notice?

"Yes. He's a great Single; best we've had so far, and I'm glad we chose him. He will be great on camera." Completely all-business textbook answer. Chicken. What she really wanted to say was…She was completely smitten with the guy. Could she trust Maggie with this info? "I'm interested to see what girls are matched to him." She added.

Because they will all be exactly like you? Maggie thought. "Me too," She thought she'd try asking, "Do you normally interact with the guys during the interview? I got the feeling from Ethan and Marcus that you don't."

"Uh...no," Claire admitted. Was she blushing? "Not usually. I don't interfere with Ethan's process. He and Marcus have a system."

"So why did you?"

"I don't know..." Claire trailed off like she couldn't think of what to say. What can I say that will appease her? Do I tell her I *like* the guy and just wanted to connect to him in some small way?

Maggie thought she would push just a little, "Do you think it's because you are discovering that he is perfect for *you*? Even I can see it," She held her hand up so Claire wouldn't answer yet. "Because I think you *like*, like him. I watched you when you first met him. You were affected by him. I saw your reaction and how you looked at him. And you put your hand on his knee just now in there. You don't do that either." Okay, maybe that was a big push. A really big one. Oh well. It was already out and said. She couldn't hit rewind.

Claire stared. How...? She couldn't think of what to say. Maggie was staring back at her waiting for an answer. "I can't believe you would think that. How did you come up with all of that? I certainly have not..." She was rambling, which was not good. Maggie could see through rambling.

Maggie was smart, and observant, and her best friend. The only one besides James who knew all about her.

Maggie said very softly, "Come on, Claire. You feel something, and you are trying to talk yourself out of it."

Claire shook her head. "This is not a conversation we can have. Andrew is on the *show*, Maggie. We are supposed to find him someone he can connect with and possibly see a future with. And it certainly *can't be ME*." Her voice got more and more frantic. "I can't believe you are saying all this."

Maggie shook her head, "Claire, I'm not just saying it. You are feeling it. What is so bad about it? You can call one of the other guys, Mike or Drake. They can take over. It's only been one day. It looks like he likes you, too. You could get to know him like any normal human." Okay, she said it. Later, she could remind Claire that she tried.

Claire suddenly got really calm and glared at Maggie. "Maggie, as I have told you over and over, I'm not interested in a relationship. Just because this guy is charming and seems to like the same things I do, *doesn't mean anything*. Please. Drop it."

"Got it, boss." Maggie relented. "Sorry." She gathered up her purse and clipboard, went over the schedule for the next day with Claire, and said goodbye. As she got on the elevator, she couldn't help but think that Claire's stubbornness was going to make for an interesting cycle, to say the least. And, good grief, it just occurred to her that this was Cycle 13. Irony.

Her phone started buzzing.

Chapter 25

"So, what do we do about *this*? Ethan said to Marcus after Andrew and the girls left the studio.

Marcus shrugged, "At least we know now why he was so weird when Claire wasn't here."

"He likes *her*." They both said in unison.

"He completely lit up when she finally spoke," Marcus observed, and Ethan nodded.

"...Which *she never does*," Ethan moved as though he was going to power off his terminal.

Marcus stopped him. "No, dude, we need to rethink the questions for tomorrow. If he likes Claire already, and he's feeling a strong connection from her as well, it will be hard to get him to focus on the girls chosen for the show. If *we* can see what's going on between them, he has to see it. We know she will fight it and be stubborn, because she doesn't believe in love for herself." Ethan could see Marcus thinking. His eyes darted and he blinked really fast. "We have two choices. We either have to tell Claire that he won't work, or we have to shift this somehow and make this secretly about Claire. She's not going to replace him after the work we put in today. So, choice #1 is out. We are going to have to orchestrate this around Claire. The success of this cycle will be in our hands, not Claire's. Because it will be about Claire.

"Can we pull this off on our own?" Ethan was smiling. He liked Claire. She deserved to be loved.

"Lemme think." Marcus did his best thinking with chocolate, so he grabbed a candy bar from the snack basket and took a big bite. "We may need Maggie," he said between chews.

"Maybe she hasn't left yet. Get her on the phone."

***

"Are you kidding me, guys, I was just leaving for the day." Maggie whined into the phone. She listened for a few second and the said, "be there in 5." She ended the call and stuffed the phone back into her purse as she got back on the elevator. The building was still full of people so it didn't feel like the end of a normal day. Entertainers never rest. There was always something happening in this building. Especially on their floors. There was always something to arrange. But she was usually home by 6 or 7. Claire would stay later sometimes, but she always let Maggie have some sort of life beyond work. She was a good boss. She had heard horror stories from other exec assistants. Glorified slaves from how they described it.

She opened the door to the interview studio to find Ethan and Marcus eating candy bars and looking like they had swallowed the cat. Or the cats that swallowed the canary... How did her mom say it? However you put it, they looked guilty of something.

"And you needed me for...?" Maggie said impatiently.

"Can we trust you?"

Maggie stared. Did she look like the most trustworthy person on the planet? Why was everyone asking her this all of a sudden? "What do you think?" She said with her hands on her hips. "This better be good."

It was good, she decided, when they finished explaining what they had discovered. She had to know how they figured it out. Two tech nerds certainly couldn't be *that* observant. They were using big words that had nothing to do with computers.

"So, tell me, fellas, how is it that you know so much about this kind of thing" She asked, "I mean, you are techies, right? Did you both minor in psych or something? Do you spend your spare time watching Dr. Phil?"

"Actually, I double majored in human behavior and marriage and family therapy." Ethan said matter-of-factly. Maggie's jaw dropped.

"And I have a master's in clinical psychology." Marcus added. "We both minored in I.T."

"And you can't tell *anyone* you know that, now. Not even Claire." Ethan said seriously.

Maggie's mouth was till wide open. That sneak. No wonder this show's process worked so well. Claire had stacked the deck. She had shrinks analyzing every move. Sneaky genius. Maggie had a new appreciation for her boss; her friend. She was smart. And doubly smart for not telling anyone.

Maggie started laughing all of a sudden. And the more she thought about it, the more she laughed. James may have broken his leg for nothing, and that thought made her laugh for some reason. Poor James. She laughed until she became conscious of the two men across the table staring at her. She needed to explain her laughter.

"S..s..sorry, guys. You have no idea what has been going on, and if you can already see the sparks between Andy and Claire, well, you need to hear the rest."

After she had explained what she knew about Andy and James and the "Plan B" that was already in motion, the three of them discussed what should be done about it.

As they were getting up to leave the room, Ethan said, "Do we need to get burner phones so we can talk about this without anyone knowing?"

Maggie and Marcus laughed and Marcus agreed it may be a good idea, but Maggie felt sure that Claire would notice another phone at some point, and she didn't want to have to explain with yet another lie. "I'm just going to change your names in my phone to different names. Margo and Theresa; my new best friends."

"I still can't believe her brother broke his leg for this."

Chapter 26

Before getting in her car, Maggie texted Claire to see if she had left for the hospital yet. Claire replied that James was at home already and that she had just brought him dinner and was about to leave his house to go home. Good. Maggie thought, she could go by and see how he was doing. Or should she? As she sat in traffic, she had a small argument with herself. The sarcastic, stubborn Maggie almost won, but the kind-hearted, romantic Maggie was victorious. Twenty minutes later, she was pulling up in front of his house.

Claire, on the other hand, was in a bad mood. James was not as injured as he had seemed at the hospital. There wasn't even a scratch on his face. He explained that some miracle cream the nurse had used had healed all the scratches. His face was red and blotchy, but there were no scratches or cuts anywhere. His arm was fine, too. He said the doctor had said it was just bruised. That was lucky, *or* was he just fishing for sympathy? She had been ignoring him for months, maybe he felt like he needed to do something drastic for her attention. That made her feel bad. And after Maggie had accosted her about Andrew, well...she wasn't in the best mood. "Why can't everyone just leave me alone!" she screamed at the car in front of her at the light.

She admitted that she was interested in Andrew. He was handsome, and smart, and charming, and unusually compatible to her. He liked the same things, thought about things in a similar way, and made her laugh. She had to fight the laughter and only laugh to herself and not out loud. But, oh, how she had wanted to. She had found herself wanting to just take over the interview and just talk to him. When he looked at her, she felt warm and vulnerable, like everyone could see through her. She liked everything about him... so far. That was the key, though, wasn't it? She didn't know everything, and in her past experience, that stuff that you discover later is always the rotten, stinky, abusive, nasty stuff that makes you never want to...

Anyway, she thought. I need to calm down and worry about tomorrow and how I'm going to get through the rest of the interview without succumbing to the "temptation" to talk to him. She laughed to herself as she had a realization. I'm going to have to endure eight weeks of watching him get to know 10 other ladies who are *just like me*. And not only watch, but orchestrate all the situations and dates. And then the finale...

She got some ice-cream out of the freezer and skipped dinner.

Chapter 27

Biggest smile EVER, Maggie thought as James answered the door and saw her standing there. He had a great smile; especially when it was directed at her. He was wearing basketball shorts and red baseball sleeves. He balanced on the crutches and swept his arm in an arc to indicate she was welcome to enter and proceed to the living room.

"I'm sorry I made you get up to get the door," she said as she walked past him. He smelled good, too. What was she doing here? "I just wanted to see if you were okay, and if you needed anything?"

"Claire brought me dinner and helped me put this thing in a big bag so I could take a bath." He paused and gave her that endearing look he was so good at, "but I could use some company to calm me down so I can sleep. I'm a little antsy. This cast is more annoying that I thought it would be, and this is only the first day." He sat down on the sofa, lifted his broken leg up on the ottoman, patted the space next to him, and looked at her with wide eyes. "Sit with me?" The room was dimly lit with only one lamp as if he were trying to relax.

She felt that flutter again. His brown eyes were captivating. "I guess I can stay for a few minutes and make sure you can rest." She sat down next to him, but not too close, and turned toward him resting her hand on the cushion between them. "I have to tell you a few things." She had decided to share a few of the things she had observed today, but not the part about Marcus and Ethan. They had decided that only the three of them would be privy to their plan. It was too risky otherwise.

"Do tell, my dear." He took her hand, and she didn't resist. He held it tenderly and familiarly as if they had done this for years. He was surprised she didn't pull away. Maybe she was starting to like him back. Could he dare hope? He had to go slow, so she could see that he was serious.

She was falling for him hard, and she knew it. She didn't know holding someone's hand could feel this wonderful. Her news just spilled out, "Claire let me sit in on the interview after lunch. She has been promising me for a while. And I'm glad it was today because I got to watch them interact. Andy really likes her. There's an electric charge between them. Killer tension. Apparently, Claire never speaks in these interviews. She just listens. But today she said something in reaction to one of his answers, and they started talking. She even leaned toward him and put her hand on his knee for a second. It was amazing."

"I knew it!" James slapped his other hand on his leg, and immediately winced in pain. "Ow..." His grip tightened on her hand for a second, and she squeezed his hand in sympathy for his discomfort, even adding her other hand for a minute. "I knew he was perfect for her."

"I tried to confront her about it briefly," Maggie added, "but she denied it and remains closed off. I think she likes him, and recognizes that he is perfect for her, but is still too afraid."

James leaned his head back on the cushion and closed his eyes. Maggie wondered out loud, "Do you need any pain medication? Tylenol? Did the doctor give you anything?"

James nodded. His leg was really aching now. "The pill bottle is on the sink in the kitchen."

Maggie got up and went into the kitchen to fetch the meds and some water. She regretted having to let go of his hand. When she returned, she sat down a little closer this time, and waited for him to open his eyes. He noticed that she sat closer. He took the medicine and handed the cup back to her. She set it on the table next to the sofa. He laid his hand open on the cushion to see if she would take it and closed his eyes again. She looked at his hand and thought, what the heck, you know you want to, and took his hand in hers. She sat back against the sofa cushion next to James so their arms were touching. She closed her eyes, too, so she didn't notice when he opened his eyes and turned his head slightly so he could look at her.

As he looked at her lovingly, he memorized everything about her face: her perfect nose, her full lips, her flawless complexion, the little freckle near her ear... He could smell her hair. He took in a long breath through his nose so he could drink in her scent. She was so close to him, it was intoxicating. He closed his eyes.

She was so comfortable she must have dozed off because all of a sudden, she was aware of him moving slightly. She opened her eyes and saw that he was asleep. His head had rolled to the side a little. His hand was still in hers, but since he was asleep it was heavy and limp. She saw the clock on the wall and was surprised to discover they had been asleep an hour or so. She slowly removed her hand from his and stood up. She took a blanket from one of the chairs and draped it over him. After writing him a short note and leaving it next to his foot on the ottoman, she quietly let herself out.

When James awoke about two hours later and got up to move to his bed, he was disappointed that she was gone, but he saw the note and smiled. "Sleep tight, Romeo."

Chapter 28

This was maddening. The more questions he answered, the more she liked him. She kept her mouth shut, though. She hadn't spoken or reacted all day. And she wasn't going to. Ethan had been asking most of the questions thus far, and they were the typical ones she was used to. Day two was usually current stuff: job, family, interests, hobbies, relationships, all the typical things you learn about a person while dating them for a long period. Andrew was a trooper. He was earnestly answering as honestly as he could, at least that she could surmise. He was just telling them about his parents and that they had just celebrated 45 years of marriage. He was in awe of his parents, whose relationship had been full of respect and mutual adoration. Each couldn't do enough for the other.

"So, how is it that you are not married?" Ethan asked. "You seem to have had a great example in your parents. You have siblings that are married.

Why not you?"

Andy looked right at Claire, but she didn't look up, so he turned his attention back to Ethan. "I have not had the privilege of finding someone who fits me...yet. My parents fit. They are interested in the same things, they laugh all the time, and they keep that spark. They don't always see eye to eye, but they respect each other, and work to keep each other interested. I don't know if that makes any sense to you. I remember the first time I wasn't grossed out by their affection for each other. I was in high school, and it was some special occasion, either Valentines or their anniversary, and my dad came downstairs in a tux. I think they were going to some fancy restaurant, and my mom got this look on her face and started talking like a teenager, saying things like,"oooh baby, you still got it," and "do I really get to go out with *you* tonight?" She looked really nice herself. Her hair was piled on top of her head and she was wearing this sexy dress... When she had come downstairs earlier, I had told her she looked hot, kind-of as a joke—I mean, you don't tell your *mom* she looks hot, right? But I remember when my dad came down and they were talking like teenagers, I was all of a sudden proud that my parents still felt that way about each other. I was just learning what it felt like to like a girl and get those butterflies and feel that attraction, and I was seeing that my parents still felt that. I was grateful that I had that example. I want that for myself. I haven't felt like that for someone, yet." He tried to look at Claire, but she wasn't moving. His look was not lost on the others in the room.

Ethan nodded, "Thanks for sharing that." Everyone in the room was touched by what Andy had just shared about his parents. Most especially Claire. She was encouraged that he had been raised in such a loving home. He had watched his parents create and nurture a good relationship. He knew what to do. It sounded like he knew how to treat a woman, because he had watched his father do it the right way for his whole life. She could feel him looking at her and wanted to look back at him, but she didn't dare. She was afraid of what she would do or say, so she kept her eyes on her notebook.

Then it all went haywire.

Marcus spoke up, "So tell me, what are your feelings about control, in a relationship?"

Andrew's eyes widened. He knew Claire's history from James. She didn't appear phased, but stayed buried in her notes. "Control in a relationship?" Andrew needed more than that. "Those words don't go together. What do you mean?"

Claire immediately recognized that this was not a typical question and was wondering the same thing. She kept her cool, though, and didn't react, even though she was feeling uncomfortable and interested at the same time.

"Well," Marcus explained. "Say, for instance, in

any of your previous relationships, has your girlfriend wanted to, say, change her hair color, or change something about herself that you were opposed to? What did you do?"

"Wow, that is quite the question." Andy knew exactly what to say, though. "I haven't exactly experienced that specific scenario in any of my relationships thus far, but I would have to say that if I had, I would have supported her in whatever made her happy."

Claire moved. She looked up at him. "Yeah, right." She said it so softly only Andy heard because he was looking right at her. He read her lips, mostly.

"Did you say something, Claire?" Andy asked. He was holding his breath, along with Ethan, Marcus, and Maggie. They had seen her lips move, too.

Claire shook her head and smiled sweetly. She looked back at her notepad and scribbled something.

He kept going, never taking his eyes off of her, "I believe that relationships should be about mutual happiness. You can't expect your partner to be happy if you are controlling all of their decisions. There is love and respect only if there is freedom and acceptance."

At the word "acceptance," Claire looked up again and stared at him while he continued.

"My dad told me once that if you love someone, you love all of them. Even the parts you may not like. You just don't focus on those parts. You focus on the parts that you love, and after a while, you don't see the other parts anymore. And you don't remember them, either. No one has the right to control another person's actions. That is just abuse. That is not a relationship."

Claire's heart was pounding and she couldn't look away. She didn't think that any man thought this way. This man who she was so hopelessly attracted to was saying all the right things. Confound it. She couldn't breathe. She had to get away. "You'll have to excuse me for a moment," she said, softly, her voice full of emotion, and she got up and left the room.

"Bingo," Marcus mouthed to Ethan behind the monitors, then he looked over at Maggie and she was staring at them with eyebrows raised. He looked at Andrew. Andrew was harder to read right then. He was looking at his hands in his lap. He had just nailed that answer, but he didn't look happy about it. Probably because it had affected Claire so deeply that she had left. He didn't want to hurt her. Marcus liked this guy more and more every minute.

Chapter 29

"I can't find her anywhere," Maggie said as she came back to the interview room. She shrugged her shoulders. She hadn't been able to find Claire. She had looked in Claire's office, the bathroom, other studio rooms, and her own office. She had walked outside and looked for Claire's car. It was still parked where it was supposed to be and Claire wasn't in it.

Marcus spoke up. "Okay people. Let's call it for today. Andrew, I believe we have enough to create a matching algorithm and start the process of choosing ten lovely ladies for you to meet." They had decided not to tell Andrew anything about their plan, yet. They didn't want to make him have to hide anything from Claire other than the fact that he was already smitten with her.

Andy nodded and clapped his hands together. "Let's get this started." He stood and shook hands with both men and nodded to Maggie, "Thank you." His look to Maggie was more of a question. He needed to speak with her, just for reassurance. He didn't like that Claire disappeared. He didn't know if that was good or bad.

Maggie got the message, "Andrew, if you'll come with me to my office, I will give you the tentative schedule for next week."

As they exited the room and headed down the hall, they missed Marcus and Ethan's elaborate high five. Two, front to back overhead slaps, an overhead slap that follows through to an underhand one, and alternating elbow slaps to a two-handed high ten; their signature sign of a job well done.

***

Claire watched Maggie come out the front of the building looking for her. She had left the studio and just walked blindly to nowhere in particular. She had gone to the corner and crossed the street at the light and ended up at the coffee shop next to the bistro across from the studio. She was sitting just back from the front window when she spotted Mags. Maggie looked worried, and Claire knew exactly what Maggie was going to say if she found her, so Claire stayed in the shadows. She was able to relax when she saw Maggie reenter the building.

She knew she had just acted in the most unprofessional way possible. She was the director for crying out loud. But she spent less time thinking about what members of her crew were thinking of her and more about the wonderful man she had "spent the day" with. He was perfect. He was kind, and generous, and honest, and stable, and confident, and...he was funny. That story about his brother's dog... she smiled and allowed herself to actually laugh this time. She had only smiled before. She had been trying so hard to keep her emotions in check that she hadn't reacted normally to anything he had said during the interview. Times when she should have laughed or reacted like a normal human, she had frozen and looked at her notebook. She didn't remember being this cold and stiff in any other interview. She usually tried to make the contestant at least feel comfortable and at ease. She was just so concerned with showing too much, that she didn't show anything.

Marcus and Ethan were freaking behaviorists. How were they not noticing her weird behavior? They hadn't mentioned it or asked what was wrong when they had all taken breaks and Andrew wasn't in the room. That struck her as odd, but she didn't dwell on it. Her mind was racing back and forth between her attraction to Andrew, and her job: finding Andrew someone to love. What a dilemma. How was she going to do this? She had wondered this same thing yesterday, and all morning, and now it was getting worse. The more she knew about him, the more she liked, and the more she could actually imagine spending time with him. He could make her days less functional and more fun. But what was she thinking? She couldn't even entertain these thoughts. She had to forge on with her job. Tomorrow she would have to watch as the computer kicked out ten names. Ten girls that were perfect on paper for Andrew. But I am perfect for him on paper, too. Number 11.

She waited at the coffee shop until she saw Andrew finally leave the building and drive away, and then made her way back to her office.

Chapter 30

"She just left. Is that normal? Did I say something wrong? What do I do now?" Andy was pacing and frantically firing questions at Maggie in her office.

Maggie grabbed his arm and shook him a little. "You did great! Are you kidding? If you hadn't killed it, she wouldn't have bolted." She indicated for him to sit.

"The rest of the week the guys will be working the computer to find the other women for your dates. Hopefully your interview time without Claire will generate some ladies who aren't attractive to you, or you to them. Then we start filming on Monday. Production has already been putting together your life story to tell the public. You will just do as you are told, pretty much. Claire is supposed to walk you through all of it, so you will have on-on-one time with her from here on out."

Maggie added, "You know, you are quite a catch. The dates you go on will probably be somewhat enjoyable. The ladies will like you even if they recognize they aren't quite compatible. Are you sure you can handle all the female attention you are going to get?"

Andy nodded. "I think so. I'll be okay. I've spent a lifetime so far looking for someone who makes me feel like Claire has...even after just these few days." He rubbed his temples. "I doubt any of them will measure up to her, so I'm not worried that there will be a challenge for me in that respect."

Maggie agreed. She really did. She could really see there was something intangible between them.

"I don't know very much about her, though. That is the only part of this I don't like very much. This is all so one sided. She knows all about me, but I don't know much about her. I was hoping she would participate more in the interviews..."

Maggie laughed. "You have no idea how much you are alike. I'm pretty sure that is why she has been so silent. She agrees with everything you have said. You have the same exact food preferences, you like the same movies, you like the same music, you are homebodies, you hate exercising, you both like football and baseball, you've both seen Wicked...shall I go on?"

"But I want to find out these things by talking to *her,* not by her listening to me drone on. I'm glad to hear I will have time with her, even if it's just little bits." Andy stood up. "I need to go clear my head." He opened the door and looked back at Maggie, "but that is almost impossible because she is always in it." He smiled weakly at Maggie and left.

Maggie felt bad for him. She really liked him. He was genuine and unassuming, and just generally pleasant to be around. She straightened up her desk and decided to text James before she left to see if he needed anything.

"Of course, my dear," he replied, "Romeo needs YOU."

She smiled and blushed. He got the note. "Do u want me to get dinner 4 u?"

"Craving grill chz and tom soup. Gonna make some right now." He smiled at the phone and hit send. Then he quickly added, "Can I make some 4 U?" and then added another text, "Please?"

She texted back quickly, "I'll be there in 30; DON'T do anything. I'll help U. Stay off your leg, dork." She hurried out the door so quickly that she didn't notice that Claire had returned.

Chapter 31

James heard her car in the driveway so he jumped up and hobbled over to greet her at the door. He waited till she stepped onto the doormat and opened the door before she could knock.

"Hello beautiful." He beamed at her.

Maggie tried not to blush, but it was difficult under the naked adoration that he was exhibiting. Had he been waiting there for her? She had to admit that she was enjoying it, but she had to make sure, "Quit the charm, Romeo. You are just glad I'm here to feed you." She was fishing and she felt only slightly guilty for it.

"Yes, I am glad you are here, but not just because you are helping me make dinner. And, no, I refuse to quit the charm. I like making you blush. You are extra lovely when you blush." He leaned toward her and kissed her cheek. Which was awkward with the crutches, but he made it happen.

She was so overwhelmed with his answer and the touch of his lips on her cheek that she almost forgot to breathe. She followed him into the living room where he plopped himself down on the sofa as she stared at him. She wanted to kiss him back. Bad.

"So, sit and tell me all about the interview today. Did you get to sit in again?" He patted the cushion next to him and gazed at her, smiling.

She sat next to him and turned to face him while he grabbed her hand. This was becoming a delicious habit. She began to tell him about how the interview was going, which she discovered was rather difficult because all the time she was talking his fingers were caressing her hand in little circles.

He listened in rapt attention, never taking his eyes off of her. Her face was so lovely and she made the cutest faces as she described what Andy had said, and Claire's abrupt departure. She was so animated. Her hand remained in his, which he found encouraging and irresistible.

"So, my sister just disappeared?" James laughed. "He must have gotten to her. GOOD for him."

Maggie looked a little concerned, "I couldn't find her. She won't answer her phone. Maybe we went too far..." Her voice trailed off and she looked far away.

"You hungry?" He asked and brought her back to him.

They got up and went into the kitchen. James hobbled, anyway. He assured her that his leg was fine and that he was sick of sitting around. They laughed together as they prepared the soup and sandwiches. When they sat down to eat at his little kitchen table, she poured them both a soda and they toasted to Claire and Andy. He wanted to toast to more than just his sister's romance, but he was moving slow. He wanted Maggie to trust him with her heart. She was too important to him now. He had decided. He wanted to be with Maggie. She made him feel all the things you are supposed to feel when you are in love. He had to make sure she knew he felt that way for only her. No one else. It had taken two years for him recognize this feeling for what it was.

When they had finished dinner, he invited her to stay again, like she had the night before. "You were magic for me last night. I haven't slept like that for a while. Will you?" James got up before she could answer and started for the other room. He looked back when she didn't get up right away. He caught her eye. Was she hesitating?

"I can stay for a few minutes and get you settled, but I fell asleep last night and stayed too late. I need to be home to do at least *some* laundry tonight." She frowned. "I'm running out of things to wear."

"Oh," He relaxed. Good. It was just laundry. "Okay then. Just a few minutes."

She hoped he wasn't just using her to fall

asleep. She hoped that he really did want her to be there with him. So much hope.

She sat down next to him like before, and this time, instead of taking her hand, he lifted his arm over her head, wrapped it around her shoulders, and snuggled her close to him. She melted into him. Her head fit perfectly in the crook of his neck, and she felt him kiss the top of her head. She could feel his breath in her hair. He smelled so good it was intoxicating. She slowly relaxed as his fingers caressed her arm ever so slightly. She found it hard to believe he would do this if he wasn't interested in her in some small way. Unless he did this with all the girls he dated. But Andy had said...

She was letting him hold her close to him. He was in heaven. Her hair smelled fantastic. He didn't think she wore a lot of perfume, but she always smelled great. He felt her breathing become more even, and her head dropped a little on his chest. She must be asleep again, he thought. He knew he should wake her, but he was enjoying this closeness to her way too much. He closed his eyes and held her for as long as he could.

Chapter 32

This was it, Claire thought. The first date. The weekend had flown by. Ethan and Marcus had been fast in locating the ladies for the show. What usually had taken two days had taken less than one, and they had been able to move up the initial first episode where Andrew is introduced and the world is able to get acquainted with him. They had filmed all of that on Friday. They were just lucky that he had gotten time off from his investment banking job. Only Maggie knew that there was no investment banking job.

Claire was more at ease around Andrew now. She was having Maggie give him instructions and the coaching that she would normally do herself. She was using the excuse that she was letting Maggie be more involved, but it honestly relieved her not to have to have too many moments with him alone. He seemed to want her around more, and Maggie told her that he asked about her all the time, and why she was there instead of Claire. "You *did* tell him that you would be with him through every step of this process." Maggie would argue more than once. Claire was stubborn. "How are you going to work your magic if you change your process?" This was the only question that made any sense to Claire, and she did consider it. She would ease into it. She would be fine.

The list of ladies was somewhat of a joke on set right now. There were three Jessicas, and two Ashleys. That had happened only once before. On Cycle 3 there were four Amys. They had had to use two middle names and a combo of first and middle. The girls drew straws to decide who got to use just Amy, so it ended up being Amy, AmyLynn, Eliza, and Marie. The running joke on set went something like this: Someone would yell out, "He's gonna choose Amy," and everyone would answer, "Which one?" Then everyone would crack up. It was just lucky that the guy eliminated two of them within the first 4 weeks. He ended up choosing AmyLynn in the end. Oh, the irony. Or the law of averages. The crew had been correct after all.

Claire had gathered all of the ladies together on Saturday morning and made them decide how they were going to work the name thing. This cycle was already different for so many reasons. The ladies didn't usually meet beforehand, but this name thing needed to be solved, so they were all in the same room. They were all mostly affable and two of the Jessicas offered to use their middle names. The Ashleys were stubborn and couldn't decide, so Claire had them play rock-paper-scissors. She had to teach one of them how to play it. This caused some confusion for Claire. How would a woman so compatible with Andrew not know how to play Rochambeau? So, after all this, it would be Jessica, (Jessica)JessLynn, (Jessica)Renee, Ashley, (Ashley)Parker, Lissette, Brittany, Emma, Lindsay, and Chloe.

The meeting with the ladies was eye-opening for Claire for a few other reasons. One reason being that none of them had graduated from college. She found that odd. She was expecting to meet ten women who were just like her, and she was not impressed to that end. The other reason was that they all seemed obsessed with their appearance. They kept asking about make-up and hair, and if they would have access to wardrobe, or did they have to wear their own clothes. They all looked like, sounded like, and acted like, teenagers. One was an actress, two were hairdressers, one was a massage therapist, and one was a pre-school teacher's aide... she couldn't go on. She was starting to wonder if she really was compatible with him. If the computer spit out this bevy of vixens as his perfect matches, then she could certainly relax, right? He shouldn't be at all interested in her.

Maggie has remarked as much, "Where did these women come from? A casting call for the

Bachelor? These are not the ladies we usually get."
She had agreed with Claire that they didn't seem
right for Andrew. Mags had also shrugged and
decided not to argue with science. Argue with
science? Is that what this was? Claire went over
and over in her head about how her show was a
mastery in the combination of research, science,
behavior, and physical chemistry. She had had such
success. It just seemed like this cycle was off the
rails somehow. Something was wrong. Something
was missing. And she couldn't put her finger on it.

Chapter 33

Maggie had barged into the computer studio Monday morning and scared the living daylights out of Marcus and Ethan. "What the heck have you done?" She screamed. "The meeting with the ladies you *chose* on Saturday was ridiculous."

Marcus started laughing, "Do you like the three Jessicas?"

"They are all so far from compatible with Andrew that it is a joke." Maggie could see that they had fun last week choosing these women. "A massage therapist? An actress? Really?"

"We thought it would be better for him and for Claire if he wasn't at all tempted." Ethan remarked. He was all business.

"What about Claire second guessing her own compatibility with him, and attraction to him, based on the girls he is matched with by the all-knowing computer?" She reasoned. "Did you think of that?"

Ethan nodded, "Yes, we thought of that, but then thought that she would ultimately be more motivated to step in and save him from them. She's going to eventually recognize that she is better for him than they are, and she is going to do something about it, because she will have fallen in love with him."

Maggie wasn't sure, but decided to trust the human behavior experts. She knew all too well what it was like to fall for someone. She had fallen for James. She thought about the past few days.

Thursday night, she had fallen asleep in his arms, and awakened after it was dark. It had even been later than the night before. He was asleep as well. Since she had been wrapped in his arms, she had to be really careful unwrapping herself so she didn't wake him. She had written another note, and left.

The next day he had texted her bright and early with a complaint and an apology. The note she left had announced that she would be unable to come by again because she had too much laundry. She stuck to her guns, but wondered if she was punishing him, or herself. She missed him, and wanted to be wrapped in his arms.

The weekend was full of the show. She had to help orchestrate the ladies, and the all their intros and bios for their dating episodes. They were a handful of drama, and she was exhausted. So, Sunday she had stayed home to finally do her laundry.

She was listening to music and it was up pretty loud while she put her last load of laundry in the dryer. She was surprised that she actually heard her doorbell ring over the music. Who could that possibly be? She thought to herself. She went to the door after turning the music down a little, and looked through the peep hole. Her heart stopped. It was James. He was on his crutches and turning to wave at a car that was driving away. He looked so handsome, flipping his hair to keep it from falling into his eyes.

She threw open the door. "What the heck, James, what are you doing here?" She was happy to see him, too happy. Calm down sister, she thought to herself.

"Hello to you, too, beautiful! I have been thinking about you nonstop, and needed to see you." James said as he hopped on one foot and put both crutches in one hand. "I've missed you. Can I come in?"

She stepped aside, and he hopped through the door and stopped to kiss her cheek like he had done before. He put his hand on the wall behind her to steady himself, and he lingered there so he could smell her hair again. His face was so close to hers. He didn't want to move. She wasn't moving either.

"I'm sorry," she said softly in his ear. "Hello...Romeo."

"Andy dropped me off. Is that okay?" He

whispered. He hadn't moved away from her. He could tell she was barely breathing.

She nodded almost imperceptibly. She looked at his lips, then up to his eyes, and she found that he was looking at her, too. They stood there for what seemed like a wonderful forever, almost touching, not wanting to break the spell. Both imagining what it would be like to...

Her phone started ringing in the other room. The spell was broken and they both walked (and hopped) into the kitchen. She answered the phone when she saw it was Claire. Maggie never took her eyes off James as she listened to Claire tell her about some changes for the next day's shoot. He returned her gaze, and sat himself down at the table, and only looked away once so he could prop his leg up on one of the other chairs. From her responses, he gathered that she was talking to his sister.

"Okay boss, I'll make sure I'm there by eight so I can brief Sid." She looked at the phone and hit the end button. "So, you really missed me?"

"I got used to you coming over every night to romance me to sleep. I haven't slept for two days." He laughed. It wasn't exactly true, but it sounded good. He was dreaming about her constantly. That was the same as not sleeping, right?

"Next time you'll be sure to respect my schedule and not let me fall asleep in your arms so irresponsibly," she laughed with him.

"Did you ever do your laundry?" And that

started them both laughing because you could clearly hear the dryer from the kitchen.

It was only three in the afternoon, so she got out a bag of potato chips and they sat at the table and talked and laughed until it started getting dark.

James offered to order a pizza, so he stayed for dinner, and then she drove him home.

When she pulled into his driveway, she turned to look at him, and tentatively asked, "Do you need me to help you fall asleep?" She was hoping he would say yes, and he did.

"Um, YES. Are you kidding?" He laughed, "I'm sure that is the silliest question you will ever ask."

She helped him into the house and got him settled on the sofa with a blanket. She was enjoying taking care of him. As long as he continued to call her "beautiful" she would do whatever he wanted. Hopefully he never figured that out.

As she was sitting down, she was reaching over him helping him adjust the cushion behind his head when she realized that he was staring at her. She was inches from his face, and she felt self-conscious all of a sudden. Before she could sit back into the sofa next to him her eyes locked on his. He leaned toward her and kissed her. His lips touched hers so tenderly and lingered there for what seemed like hours. The magic from when he kissed her cheek earlier was back in full force. She kissed him back, tasting his lips and feeling his breath. She trembled, and he responded with a little more urgency.

He was making her tremble and that was encouraging. Maybe she isn't flirting anymore. Maybe this is real for her, too. Their lips parted slightly as they continued kissing. After a minute, he pulled away slightly and looked into her eyes. "I've wanted to do that for a long time."

"Me, too." Her voice was shaking. She leaned into him and kissed him again, this time while snuggling up to him as he wrapped his right arm around her and pulled her close and cradled her face with his left hand.

After a few minutes of the most satisfyingly glorious kiss of her life, she buried her head into his neck and totally relaxed. He laid his head back on the sofa and stroked her hair.

As he felt her relax and doze off, he said softly, "I'm falling in love with you, Maggie."

As she slipped into sleep, she thought she heard him say something, but it sounded so far away. She only heard her name.

Chapter 34

Ashley, the hairdresser, was the first date. The girls' names had gone in a hat for a random drawing for date order. The format for the show was simple. Unlike other popular dating reality shows, the participants did not all live in a big house together and party all the time. On Single No More, each of the ladies got individual dates with Andrew. This first-date segment took about six days to film. Because some of the dates were during the day or in the morning, they could film two dates in one day.

Claire had spent the entire weekend planning the dates that each of the girls would have with Andrew. She got all of her ideas from the notes she took during the interviews with Andrew. Ashley and Andrew would be attending a Dodger game that evening. The morning was all about pre-date interviews with Andrew and the girls that were slated for the next 4 dates.

Maggie was in a happy daze all morning and Claire needed her to focus. "MAGS!" She snapped.

Maggie startled and almost spilled her drink. "Sorry boss... didn't get a lot of sleep last night."

"What is the deal with that? That has been your excuse since last Friday." Claire looked down at her notes.

"Actually, I..." Holy cow she almost said it out loud. "It's nothing. I just started seeing someone and it's been kind of a whirlwind." Maggie decided to be honest for most of it. But there was no way she was telling Claire that she was kissing her brother last night. Not yet, anyway.

"What?" Claire stared. "You didn't even tell me you were going on a date."

"It happened really fast, and you've been so swamped." Maggie offered. "I didn't want to distract you from getting ready for this week."

"That is great!" Claire gave her a hug.

"I'm really falling for this guy, and I think he said he was falling in love with me last night, but I can't be sure because I was half asleep when he said it." Maggie blushed. She may have said too much.

"After a WEEK!" Claire was in shock. "Wait a minute, Mags. You are in love after knowing a guy less than a week?

She was in too deep now so she thought she'd deflect it onto Claire, "Well, it *IS* possible, Claire, you know...to fall for someone that quickly. It has been known to happen. But, in truth, I've actually known him considerably longer than a week. We just kind-of connected in a deeper way in the last few days." She looked at her clipboard and changed the subject. "It looks like we have the Ashley pre-date interview in 10 minutes. We should get in there."

Claire was still staring at her as she walked out of the office and down the hall toward the interview studio. Maggie's got me there, she thought. She had fallen for Andrew in a few days. She physically shook that thought out of her head and followed behind Maggie.

Ashley was sitting in the interview bay. The cameras were not visible to her. Claire had learned that people were more self-conscious with those big cameras, so she used really small one-way mirrors and potted plants to hide them. The subjects consciously knew the cameras were there, they just weren't in their faces. They spoke more naturally and readily that way.

"Is my make-up okay?" Ashley was squinting up at the lights and looking at herself in the mirror to her left.

Maggie was reassuring her that she looked beautiful. Claire was letting Maggie do the interview today. Maggie had watched Claire do them for years.

"Now, I will ask you the questions, and you just answer naturally, and look right at me." Maggie smiled at Ashley. "Remember, don't look at the cameras, or talk to the cameras. Talk to me. We are just having a conversation like two girls getting ready for a date. Okay?"

"I think so," Ashley looked at herself in the mirror again and straightened her blouse. And Maggie looked back at Claire and made a face.

Claire gave Maggie a thumbs-up and said, "Rolling" to no one in particular. All her crew had on ear buds so they could hear whatever she said. She watched the monitor that was set up next to her director chair.

"So, Ashley, how do you feel about meeting Andrew?" Maggie got right to it.

"Ohmygosh, I am, like, so excited. He just looks so cute and handsome. I can't wait. Do you, like, know where we are going on the date? Is it somewhere romantic? I'm just, like, really excited and, like, really nervous." This all came out quickly in what sounded like one sentence.

Maggie tried not to laugh. "Ashley, you need to speak more slowly."

"Oh, sorry, I'm just excited. This is, like, my first time doing something like this. I, like, want to make a good impression. I, like, want him to like me."

"Nine." all the crew heard Claire say it, and they were all trying not to laugh. Ashley had just said "like" nine times in 20 seconds. Only two of the times were legitimate reasons for using the word. "Like" was one of Claire's pet peeves.

Maggie knew she had to get her to stop saying it. "I know you are nervous and excited, but you need to try not to say "like" all the time. Can you try it?"

"Umm." Ashley looked confused. "Like, I don't know what you mean."

"I'll give you an example. Like, when you, like, talk, you, like, tend to, like, say like, like every other word."

"Oh. Like, do I really do that?" Ashley was still visibly confused.

Maggie hoped, but wasn't at all confident, that she could pull this off.

Chapter 35

Ashley was a disaster, thought Claire. Maggie had done her level best, and Claire could not fault her in any way. She was also not confident that they would be able to edit that interview into something coherent. Maybe they could get some candids at the game.

They were in the van on the way to the stadium. Claire had purchased a block of seats near third base that backed up to a wall, so that there would be no one sitting behind the couple. It was just easier that way and the box office was familiar with her request now. They had shot numerous dates at games in the last few years. Looky-loos were the bane of the TV reality director's existence. People wanted to be on TV and would do strange things to get their face on screen. One year a group of teenage boys sitting behind their couple had taken off their shirts and gyrated around for a few minutes. She had had to scrap the entire dialog during the gyration.

The stadium knew they were coming and allowed them to park right at the 3rd base entrance gate. As the crew unloaded, she chuckled as she remembered what had happened about an hour ago when they filmed Andrew picking up Ashley and her "home." They never filmed at someone's actual residence. For Ashley, Claire chose a "house" facade on the studio lot that looked like a condo. Andrew's face when he first saw Ashley was priceless. It was a mixture of emotions: shock, incredulity, graciousness, and a little confusion. Because Claire felt like she knew him really well now, she could tell he was trying to be nice, but not quite sure what to do. Ashley had chosen to wear the most ridiculous outfit. She wasn't told the date location, but Maggie had told her to dress for casual outdoors. She came to the door in three-inch stilettos and a skin tight, sleeveless floral dress. She wore it well, no question. But it was so inappropriate for outside casual. She was dressed to go clubbing. The floral print was also really bright and loud. Almost clown-like.

Ashley had also planted a big kiss on his cheek before she even said "hello," leaving a big lipstick mark on his face. Claire was going to have to edit like crazy. Claire had handed him a face wipe after he put Ashley in the passenger seat, and was walking around the car to get in on the driver side, and they had shared a knowing laugh. He had given her a "help me" look. He was clearly uncomfortable with Ashley. She wasn't sure if she should feel sorry for him, since the computer used his profile to choose Ashley, but she did anyway. It was just too comical of a match to be real.

Claire spotted the car coming toward them before anyone else. "Places, people. Here they come."

Terry was the "camera in the car." She fit better in the back seats than Mark or Sid, and was better at being invisible. There were small cameras on the dashboard as well, which filmed most of what they usually used in editing, but Claire liked having another person with the couple the whole time. It helped with the shows image that there was a "chaperone" always present. Not that any of her contestants had ever gone rogue and been inappropriate, but she felt better having someone she trusted there at all times, even if just for emergencies.

As the car came to a stop, Terry continued filming from inside the car, as Mark and Sid approached from both sides to capture every possible angle. Andrew jumped out of the car and ran around the front of the car to open the door for Ashley. She didn't wait for him and he barely missed getting hit by her door.

Terry jumped out of the back seat and immediately found Claire. "Boss, she has not stopped talking...and her voice... I need an aspirin." She rubbed her forehead and the bridge of her nose. "I'm pretty sure Andrew will need an aspirin as well."

Claire watched Andrew help Ashley out of the car. He had offered her his hand, and she didn't let go of his hand and arm, or stop talking until they got to their seats. This included the entire walk around the concessions to decide what they wanted to eat, and to buy some Dodger gear to wear. Ashley refused to wear the cap he bought for her even though she had chosen it, because it would mess up her hairdo. And she refused to eat anything because she was on a gluten free, no carb diet at the moment, and "the nitrites in those hot dogs would make me sick," She had declared this a little too loudly as they made their way down to the seats. She didn't need the camera crew following her to attract attention. She was an entertaining attraction all on her own.

Andy purchased two Dodger Dogs and had eaten one of them before they even got to their seats. He was in endure-mode...just trying to make it through the evening. This woman was the most tiring person he had ever been around. She talked incessantly about everything and nothing. He was amused by the outfit she had chosen, because it was so outlandish. It was all he could do not to laugh every time he looked over at her or even thought about it. Whenever possible, he tried to catch Claire's eye. She had to see how ridiculous this date was. She had to see that he had no interest in Ashley.

Claire was enjoying the game. She had eaten her Dodger Dog already, and an entire bag of peanuts. Kershaw was pitching, and the sun was setting behind them. The sunset colors were streaming through the portals. Dodgers were up 4-0. It was a beautiful night. She sat a few rows in front of her production so that she could be aware of, but not a part of, the date. She had to give them space, even though there were two cameras right in their faces and a third a little further away for game shots and perspective shots. She tried not to look around and be obvious, but she didn't need to. Ashley never stopped talking, so Andrew never uttered a word.

Sometime in the bottom of the 7th inning, Ashley, all of a sudden, stood up and declared that she needed to use the ladies' room. Claire motioned for Terry to follow her, and both women climbed up the stairs toward the restroom. Sid put down his camera and Andy put his head in his hands. Sid said something to him, put his hand on his shoulder in a gesture of male solidarity, and got up to stretch.

"Go ahead and take a break, Sid," Claire said softly. Only Sid, Terry, Mark, and Adam—the sound tech, could hear her in their ears. "We may call this one early. We aren't going to get much more. Terry, see if you can get her to say anything meaningful."

Sid walked up the stairs to stretch his legs, just as they announced that Bellinger was up. Claire sat forward and realized that there was a man on first, no outs. "Come on, Cody!!" She yelled. There was a movement to her left and suddenly Andrew was sitting next to her. He had hopped over the rows of seats between them. She looked surprised, but didn't object. They watched in silence for two pitches and then Andy spoke, "I don't think I need another date with Ashley. She is a nice girl, but definitely not for me. We have different goals, and a vastly different fashion sense."

Claire started laughing and couldn't stop. Andy loved her laugh and it was contagious. He had only meant to be slightly funny, maybe even just sarcastic, but she was cracking up. He began chuckling just at her attempts to stop laughing, and then it turned into a trade of sorts. She would start to calm down, and his laughs would get stronger, and he would make some comment about Ashley's outfit. She mentioned Ashley's shoes, and then he said something about a clown. She had tears streaming down her face at one point, and was clutching his arm. When they finally settled and looked back at the game, Bellinger was on second and Barnes was on first. They had missed some action. No more laughing, now. The bases were loaded, and Justin Turner was up. Claire's favorite.

All around them fans started cheering and standing up, so they both stood up and started cheering. Turner swung at the first pitch and missed. Strike one. The second pitch was low and outside. Ball one. The third pitch, CRACK, the ball sailed toward the left field wall. Going... going... GONE. GRANDSLAM. Claire and Andy yelled and quite naturally jumped up and down and into each other's arms in a big hug like they had been coming to these games and cheering together for years.

It was so right and felt so good to hold her even in the midst of the frenzy of the game. He let go of her quickly so she wouldn't freak out, and they both got quiet as they stared at each other. Her eyes were full of conflict, but which side would win?

As she finally looked away from him and looked awkwardly around at the cheering fans, the sounds in the stadium were deafening, but she could hear nothing but her own heartbeat. She felt that he could probably hear it, too.

Andy knew he had to do something that would help her relax. He could see the uncertainty in her movements. He didn't want her to run again. "Hey, Claire," smiling broadly, he raised his right hand for a high five and continued, "Whooo, what a hit! Now we are up by eight! YES."

She hesitated, and he called her on it, "Don't leave me hanging, girl!"

She raised her hand and smiled. Instead of just hitting his hand, she hung on to it for a fraction of a second longer than a typical slap and looked him in the eye. She wanted him to know that she recognized his attempt to lighten the moment a little. Then she turned toward the field and they both continued clapping and cheering as Turner rounded third and trotted into home plate where the other runners were waiting to congratulate him.

That was harmless enough, Claire thought.

That was incredible, Andy thought.

That was interesting, Mark thought. As the remote cameraman, he was seated in the section of seats about 20 yards below and to the left of Andy and Claire, and he continued to point his zoom camera directly at them.

Chapter 36

Sid was the last to arrive at the secret meeting. Well, it wasn't *that* secret, but it was just for the members of the crew that Ethan had determined needed to know. So that included the cameras, lighting, editing, sound, and Maggie.

It was early Wednesday morning. Way earlier than Maggie had thought Claire might arrive. Claire could not catch a bunch of her crew leaving a meeting that she had no knowledge of. There had been some groans at the early call, but they were sufficiently curious. Mark had his own ideas.

Marcus and Ethan had arranged the chairs in a circle so everyone would feel included and free to share their thoughts.

Sid grabbed a donut from the side table, and sat down. "Sorry, there was extra traffic on the 10 west. Go figure." They all rolled their eyes and nodded or groaned in solidarity. The occupational hazard of working anywhere in L.A. was traffic. The studio was in Century City, so anyone who lived east of there, which was most of the crew, and most of the general population for that matter, was always waiting in a slow-moving lane on one of the freeways. Sid lived in Monterey Park, so he had to crawl through downtown to get to work.

Ethan spoke first, "Thank you for coming. This is important. Maggie, Marcus, and I have been working on something that we think you should know about and hopefully help with.

"But if you are uncomfortable in any way, there is no obligation to stay or be included." Marcus added seriously. This was an organized mutiny of sorts and he didn't want anyone to feel like they were coerced when it came time for Claire to fire all of them if it went south.

"What the heck, Marcus! What does that mean?" Terry leaned forward in her chair.

Marcus and Ethan looked at each other. This could be harder than they thought.

"Okay, here goes," Ethan started. "I'm just going to throw this out there and feel free to jump in at any time..."

"COME ON," They all yelled.

Ethan began to outline all that had transpired during the Andrew interviews. He expressed his professional opinion and then admitted what he and Marcus had done to choose the girls.

There were multiple comments offered regarding the girls. They were all in agreement that they were amazed and confused by them. Terry laughed, "After yesterday, I was going to come in here today and tell you that something was very wrong with the computers."

"Yeah, I was thinking they were sick or something. You know, a virus?" Sid added.

"Hardee har har." Marcus rolled his eyes.

Marcus then told them all about their plan to flip the narrative on Claire. "We think she likes him back, but will not dare interfere with the show."

"Plus the fact that she doesn't think the 'love thing' applies to her. I can tell she's fighting it. Her biggest obstacle is her." Maggie added.

They were all aware of Claire's philosophy about her own love life. They had all at one time or another tried to fix her up with one of their friends.

"There's no way she thinks these girls are legit," Terry said seriously. "I mean, she's not stupid."

"We have done four interviews so far, and only one of those four, Jessica, is anywhere near compatible with Andrew, and that is still an Elasta-girl stretch for sure." Maggie offered. "Claire hasn't said *one word* to me about it. She's not operating in her normal way. I think she is so self-conscious about her feelings toward him that she won't bring up anything that will cause her to have to talk about him in any meaningful way. She's afraid of being discovered."

"Too late." said Sid. "*She's* not stupid, but she must think *we* are."

Mark raised his hand. "I have already noticed certain things...awkward behavior from the two of them, by the way. I have footage."

"Really?" Marcus wasn't surprised, per se, but wasn't aware there may already be film.

"Yep," Mark continued. "She usually has us continue rolling whether or not she cuts the scene, so at the game on Monday, when the girl went to use the facilities, Claire sent Terry with her, and gave Sid a stretch break. She never told me to stop, so I kept on Andrew like I normally would. He left his seat and moved to sit next to Claire and they watched the game right before the grand slam. They were even laughing hysterically at something at one point. When the ball went over the wall, they both jumped up and hugged. Then I could tell it got weird...awkward...for Claire, but Andrew fixed it somehow and they continued watching together till Sid came back, and Andrew went back to his seat. Then yesterday, at the Aquarium with the one called Lissette, I caught them right after the girl excused herself to take a phone call—that lasted for 15 minutes by the way. We were outside by the penguin exhibits. Claire had Terry tail the girl. Sid and I stayed with Andrew. Andrew motioned for Claire to come look at something, and they stood there laughing about who knows what until the girl returned. It's good stuff, I mean, he would lean over close to her like he was whispering in her ear. I got it all."

Sid laughed, "I got some of that, too. Thought it was normal stuff, but now that I *know*..."

Mark continued, "Then last night at the rescue

mission, when the girl, Brittany, refused to wear
the gloves to serve the food because she had just
gotten her nails done, and pretended to need to
use the ladies' room, Claire had to step in and help
Andrew serve the food and I got some really nice
moments there. Isn't that Brittany girl the one who
is a nurse's assistant? I mean, really. If we can't get
Claire to let her hair down and relax, we could
definitely edit this cycle into a comedy segment full
of date bloopers. I mean, really. It *IS* Cycle 13 after
all."

Everyone laughed.

"And you're sure there's film?" Ethan asked.
"Bill?"

Bill, the editor tech, shrugged. "I haven't gone
through any of the three dates, yet. I was waiting
for Claire."

"FANTASTIC." Ethan jumped up and started
pacing. "Okay, here's what I propose. Bill, you need
to find that footage and copy it somewhere, and
delete it from the main footage, or whatever you
call it. So, when you and Claire do the editing, she
doesn't see it. And you need to continue to do that
for any more that comes in that involves her and
Andrew."

"We could tell Bill when we know we have
caught them on tape, so he isn't wasting a bunch of
time." Terry offered, nodding at Mark and Sid for
consent. They both nodded back.

"And then Maggie, Marcus and I will come in
and do separate editing on just the Andrew/Claire

film." Ethan added. "Any other ideas?"

"Have we thought any further beyond simply filming them interacting?" Mark asked.

Everyone looked at each other with eyebrows raised.

"Clearly not?" Mark chuckled. "Okay, how 'bout this? We will keep filming and editing, and in a few weeks if there is still a spark between them and we can tell if it has grown at all, or whatever, we will reconvene and figure it out."

Everyone nodded.

"Agreed." Ethan clapped his hands together and then said, "Don't do anything different. Don't try to help it along. Let her figure it out. We will just observe."

Maggie's phone buzzed. "It's Claire. She's on her way. I should go get her bagel."

"Hands in?" Marcus put his hand in the circle. They all followed suit. "Andrew and Claire on three. One. Two. Three."

"Andrew and Claire" They may have said it too loud, but it was 7am. No one who mattered was in the building, yet.

Chapter 37

"Are you coming over tonight? Mom is back and is coming to clean this place because I am lame and she feels pity, and she is asking about you. Have you been avoiding her?" James was leaving a message for Claire. It was Wednesday morning and he assumed she was on her way to work, and wasn't picking up because she was driving. "Call me, sis. Mom and I need some Claire time. Tonight." He hit end and put his phone down and closed his eyes. Then he picked it up again and texted Maggie. "Can u come over tonight? Please, please? My mom will be here. Have u met her?" He hit send.

He laid his head back to rest it on his headboard. All these women in his life. His driven sister, his crazy mom, and his beautiful Maggie. At least he was hoping she was his or would be. He wracked his brain trying to remember if Maggie had been at anything in the past few years where she would have met his mom. Maybe?

Had she heard him say he was falling in love with her? Had he said it too softly? Was she already asleep? She hadn't reacted, and she hadn't left a note that night when she left. Was that a sign? He needed to be straight with her. He couldn't play around. But he was starting to get nervous about it. She had kissed him back. That memory was still on his lips. If he closed his eyes, he could still feel her lips there, and feel her breath, and smell her hair.

She hadn't been able to come over the last two nights. She was in production all Monday and Tuesday while the rest of them were filming the first and second dates. Andy had corroborated that she wasn't at the stadium or the aquarium. She said she had to help edit the interviews with the first four girls. Claire was giving her more to do this time, which she was stoked about, but it meant more time at work. She had told James that she thought Claire was trying to distance herself from the girls Andy would be dating. Claire hadn't done any of the interviews. She was on set, directing, but not interviewing like she usually did. Something subconscious, probably. Maybe?

James started to laugh out loud remembering what Andy had told him last night about his last three dates. The girls were out-of-this-planet ridiculous. There could never be three women he had less in common with. They both agreed that getting Claire out of the interview had worked; maybe too well. One had never stopped talking and had worn the most outlandish outfit, and one had worn all black with no make-up and didn't talk at all, until she had gotten a phone call, and then was gone for a really long time. Andy had used that time to interact with Claire.

The last one was the funniest. She was supposed to be a nurse's assistant; which would lend you to believe that she could handle gross things, and liked to help people. Any normal human would come to that conclusion, yes? So, Claire had arranged for them to go to the rescue mission and help serve dinner, and then go out for ice-cream. When she found out where they were going, she had flipped out. She refused to wear the gloves to serve the food. "MY NAILS. OMG. I just had them done, and no WAY am I putting them in those nasty gloves." James could still hear Andy's spot-on impression of her surfer accent. Andy didn't care because that meant that Claire had to jump in and help him while Miss Acrylic sat off to the side and tried not to touch anything. He told James that he was just enjoying the opportunities to talk to Claire. Nothing fancy, nothing profound. Just real.

James agreed that it was a good strategy. Little by little. Chip away at the wall. "Don't go all Pink Floyd on her." James had said. That got a good laugh from Andy, and they had started chanting,

"Tear down the wall, tear down the wall."

His phone notified him there was a text from Maggie. He could tell immediately it was from her. He had set his notification for Maggie to a few bars of his favorite old-school love song, so when Dennis DeYoung started singing, "You know it's you, babe," he quickly picked it up and read her answer.

"I may be able to make it tonight. I'm almost done with the third girl, so I only have one more. Today should be enough. What time?"

Before he could answer, a text came in from Claire. No special notification tone for her. She almost never texted him. Maggie usually did all of that for her. "I call mom all the time, u brat. Just not since she got back. I think I can tonight, because the date for today is during the day. Tonight's had to be rescheduled."

"You know it's you, babe…" played again. "I met your mom last year at Claire's b-day. How are u explaining my presence at this obviously family dinner?"

James thought for a moment. Oh yeah. Ummm. He hadn't thought this through. He just wanted her there. He couldn't tell her he wanted her to be his official girlfriend with a text. That would be a garbage move. He had to be thoughtful and romantic about it. But how was he supposed to do that before dinner?

"You know it's you, babe..." He was taking too long to answer and she was probably wondering why. "You know, I can just come up with an excuse to need to ask Claire about something, and just show up because I know she's there, and you can just invite me to stay?" she offered.

It was a good plan, but he really wanted her there as his girlfriend. He was excited to show his mom that he had finally found someone. "Okay, let's go with that. Good thinking." He replied, adding a few heart emojis.

He would keep thinking.

Chapter 38

Good thinking. Yeah. I'm a good thinker, Maggie thought as she put her phone down. His lag in response time bugged her a little. But then, maybe it was because he wanted her to be there on purpose and not an afterthought and he was trying to figure out how to do that. Now, she reasoned, I could be negative and upset about him being thoughtless, or I could be positive and believe that he wants something more, but needs time to figure it out. Oh boy.

She had spent the last two full days and nights trying to make sense of four crazy interviews that she had no idea how to spin in a positive manner. She had been sitting in on editing now and then for the last three years with Claire, but Claire had had normal subjects to deal with. Complete sentences. She had never met this many women who had so much trouble speaking in complete, coherent sentences. She and Bill had spent a long two hours on 15 minutes of film yesterday alone, and that was 15 total minutes. Not 15 minutes after the edit. There was only 15 minutes' worth of film on Ashley that made any sense. It took them two hours to slice and dice to create about eight minutes of an interview. Maggie had had to call and arrange quick interviews with a handful of family and friends of all four girls just to lengthen each interview to the 20 minutes they usually allowed for on the show.

Now, mind you, she wasn't dogging the girls. They were actually very nice girls. They were trying really hard. She liked Lissette. Lissette was just painfully shy. The camera loved her. She was lovely… just mute.

Bill was helping, but she was starting to feel overwhelmed. She appreciated Claire giving her more to do, but she didn't have the experience to handle what was being thrown at her. She was going to have to tell Claire that she was drowning.

Claire poked her head in her doorway, "Hey Mags, I need you in editing. Bill wants to show me what you have so far." She disappeared before Maggie had the chance to answer.

"Here goes," She groaned.

***

"That's all you have?" Claire had her hands on her hips as she stood behind Bill in the editing room. Maggie couldn't read her expression.

As Bill and Maggie nodded their heads slowly, Bill spoke, "it's not Maggie's fault. If you want, I can show you the raw footage to prove that this is all we have because it is all we were given."

"There were only 15 minutes of original film on Ashley. You were in the room. She was the "like" girl." Maggie added.

"I think we can work with it," Bill said, "because Maggie got some family and friends interviews done last night and Monday night that we can add in."

"We were going to finish them today." Maggie smiled weakly. "Just let me know if you think I'm in over my head, and you can take over. I won't be offended. I promise." She looked hopefully at Claire. Hoping she would let her off the hook and take over.

Claire was upset that the girls were giving Maggie such headaches. But she didn't want anything to do with getting to know these girls in any intimate way like she usually did. She wanted to be as far away from them as possible. It was bad enough that she had to go on the dates with them, but watching them with Andrew was getting harder. The fact that they were so obviously *not right* for him made it even worse. None of them were like her in any way. It was encouraging that he didn't seem interested in any of the first three, but that didn't mean that among the next seven, there wouldn't be one or two that he would like.

The computer was never wrong. She had 12 cycles of success to prove it.

"No, I think you have done remarkably well. Keep up the good work." Claire smiled at both of them, patted Bill on the shoulder, and left the room to their collective amazement.

"Like I told you," Maggie stood up. "She doesn't want anything to do with these girls."

Bill nodded.

"You and I are going to have to tough it out." Maggie headed for the door. "I will be back in about 30 minutes to start on the family interviews. Don't go away."

"Right," Bill laughed, "Like, where, like, would I, like, go?"

Chapter 39

"Maggie," One of the interns poked her head in the door. "There's a delivery for you in your office."

Maggie looked up from the monitor to see the intern disappear and close the door. She and Bill had been working nonstop for four hours. It was past time to break for a quick lunch, but neither wanted to leave without finishing the interview they were minutes away from finishing. That would mean only one more after lunch and they would be done with all four.

"What did she say?" Maggie rubbed her eyes and looked blearily at Bill, who took a spin around on his chair. It was how he got his cobwebs out.

"You," He tried to point at her as he spun around, "have a delivery in your office?"

"Good gravy." She stood up. "Should we just finish after some food? I'm getting loopy."

Bill stood up, too. "Yep. See you in, what 30?

45?"

"30." She ran her fingers through her hair. "Let's get this done. I have dinner plans that I want to actually make tonight."

They parted in the hall and Maggie took the stairs up to her office.

When she got close to her office, there were a few people milling around her office door. When she came into view, they all grinned at her and then slowly moved away from her door.

This delivery must be interesting, she thought, to draw such a crowd.

She opened her door and was accosted by the intoxicating scent of roses. There were at least ten dozen red roses adorning her desk in various vases. They completely blocked the entire area behind her desk, including her chair.

"OH MY GOSH!" She threw her hands up to her cheeks and just stared with her mouth wide open. Her heart was beating wildly. No one had *ever* sent her flowers like this before. She started repeating, "OH my gosh, OHMYGOSH, oh my GOSH, Oh. My. Gosh. AAAAA!" Then she started laughing, which turned into tears, as she slowly moved forward to smell the bouquet closest to her. She leaned in to smell the blossoms, and her nose became aware of different scent.

James.

She inhaled sharply as something moved behind her desk. Her heart stopped.

James.

He stood up slowly from where he had been sitting low in her chair-- out of sight. He was holding one single rose in his hand, and looking at her sheepishly. He slowly smelled the rose, and then held it out to her as she walked around her desk, took the rose and kept going straight into his arms.

She couldn't stop the tears now. She held him so tightly; she hoped she wasn't hurting him. She nuzzled her face into his neck and they began to sway. He shifted while they swayed so he could lean on the edge of the desk. "Oh James." She whispered into his neck. "This is the most beautiful thing anyone has ever done for me."

"Beautiful flowers for my beautiful Maggie." He murmured into her ear.

"*Your* Maggie?" She pulled her head back to look up at him through her tears. "Am I *your* Maggie?"

She didn't want to let go of him, but he moved her away from him just enough to reach up with both hands to hold her face. He looked into her eyes with all the love in the world. "I don't know if you heard me the other night because you were falling asleep, so I'll say it again." He closed his eyes and took a breath. When he opened his eyes, her eyes met his with encouragement. "I'm falling in love with you, Maggie."

Maggie leaned into him and softly kissed him. Her hands were on his chest and she could feel his heart beating. So, she hadn't imagined it. He *had* said it on Sunday night. She was in heaven. She didn't think it was possible to feel this wonderful.

His lips left hers after a while and moved to kiss her ear and then her neck. His arms went around her waist.

"It took you long enough," she put her arms around his neck, "I've been in love with you for years."

He pulled his head back and looked at her incredulously. "Wait...What? Why didn't you say...?" He stuck his lower lip out and feigned a pout. "Maggie. I flirted with you endlessly. You never flirted back. How was I supposed to know?" He couldn't believe it. She was right there the whole time; waiting for him to get a clue.

Still in a close embrace, she moved her right hand to point a finger right in his face. "You were always with another girl." Then she traced his lips with her finger and whispered, "I didn't want to be just another girl."

He kissed her again, and in the middle of the kiss he whispered, "Never."

Chapter 40

Claire pulled up to James' house. There was already a car in the driveway so she parked on the street. She had a fleeting thought that Maggie had a car like that, but she was so distracted by what was happening in her life that it didn't connect. She just assumed her mom had gotten a different car. She talked with her mom weekly, but they didn't meet up that often. Claire was always busy, and Mrs. Culver had her own successful business as a CPA. James and Claire's father had passed eight years ago, and in the last few years she had begun traveling with her ladies' group. If she wasn't working, she was taking selfies of herself standing in front of some famous monument or landmark. Last month it was Mt Rushmore, but the month before that it was the Leaning Tower of Pisa, and she had just returned the day before from a trip to San Francisco.

Poor Claire was not in a good mood. Today she had endured yet another of the dates she had arranged. Then she was forced to watch the final edits of the four girl interviews only an hour ago. She had to admit, though; Maggie and Bill made the girls look good. She could not figure out why she was feeling so angry lately. Her thoughts, more often than not, were not where they should be. She had lost focus. She was usually fired up at this point in the process. It was her favorite part of directing this show. She loved orchestrating the dates. She fancied herself rather clever at nailing the perfect spots for the dates, and usually felt the same anticipation of possible romance that she hoped the contestants were feeling. For the most part she used the guy's preferences, because ultimately, it was easier to plan that way. He was the one choosing, so he should be able to see the ladies' behavior in his own element. It sounded heavily one sided when she tried to explain it to someone, but it worked.

It wasn't working this time. She wasn't feeling the same anticipation. It was more like a feeling of dread. She would never admit that it was because she was attracted to Andrew. Nope. Don't say it. Don't think it. Don't feel it, and it will eventually go away. She had decided to blame it on the crazy girls that they had met so far. That is what it was-- definitely.

This date had been slightly better than the first three, so that spoke volumes. The girl, Renee—one of the Jessicas—was a barista at a coffee shop in the Valley. She was actually endurable. She had been dressed appropriately and wasn't whiney about what they did. Andrew had mentioned in his interview that his family was into See's candy, so she had arranged for a tour of the original candy factory in Los Angeles. Andrew had enjoyed himself at the factory, making friends with all of the candy makers on the tour. After the first three date disasters, Claire was expecting Renee to announce that she was either allergic to peanuts or on a chocolate free diet, but Renee was affable and seemed to enjoy herself. Claire noticed that Renee would hold Andrew's arm whenever she could. It bothered her and she couldn't shake it, but Claire noticed and appreciated that he would find ways to extricate himself from Renee's hold in ways that did not appear obvious to anyone but Claire.

At one point, Renee had gotten chocolate on her shirt while she and Andrew were "helping" at the caramel table. One of the candy makers had quickly taken her to one of the sinks along the wall to help her wash it out. While Renee was gone, Andrew had beckoned to Claire to join him at the table to ask her a question, but when she got close, he picked up a fresh chocolate caramel that was still dripping and insisted she try it. "It's my favorite. I want you to try it." Before she knew it, the caramel was in her mouth, and there was chocolate dripping down her chin. She lifted her hand to wipe the chocolate off, but before she could get there, Andrew stopped her with one hand, pulled his food safety glove off the other with his teeth, and used his now gloveless hand to gently and slowly wipe the chocolate drips away...his fingers lingering a little too long near her lips while he looked directly into her eyes. "Oops, sorry," he had said, with a low chuckle, "I thought the chocolate had dried." She had laughed as well, saying something dumb about how the candy was yummy, so it didn't matter.

She was oblivious to the three cameras that were still trained on Andrew...and her. Nor did she notice the looks on the faces of her camera operators as they glanced at each other.

Now, in front of James' house, she tried to shake the anger and the other feelings in the pit of her stomach that she couldn't really explain as she got out of her car and strode up the brick walkway.

She knocked on the front door, turned the knob, and then walked in. "Door's unlocked again, James," She yelled into the house. "I've told you repeatedly just because your community is gated doesn't mean..." She stopped talking as she entered the kitchen and saw Maggie standing at the kitchen counter cutting vegetables. James was standing behind her and his arms were wrapped tightly around her waist, and his head was resting on her left shoulder. Maggie was giggling.

They both looked at her and smiled. Well, James smiled. Maggie's smile was less confident.

Claire looked right at Maggie as she quickly put

two and two together. "You were talking about my BROTHER!?"

James turned his head toward Maggie to see her face, "You were *talking* about me?" He asked with a twinkle in his eye.

Claire stared at Maggie. She was trying to keep it together. She wished that one of them would have at least warned her, so she could have been prepared. She felt like screaming and she didn't know why. There was no logical reason for her to feel this betrayed. Her brain was cheering but her heart hurt. Maggie was actually perfect for James. She had tried for the last few years to invite Maggie to family events so they could get to know each other, and when nothing had happened, well, she had just given up. So, why did their cozy embrace bother her?

Claire's voice was quiet and a little shaky and directed at her brother, "She said she thought she heard you say you were in love with her." She was fighting to keep it even.

"I did." James said. "And I am." He squeezed Maggie tighter and kissed her ear, as she blushed and smiled.

Maggie could tell that Claire was about to lose it. She tried to think of something to do to break the tension that she could see taking over Claire's whole being. She was white as a sheet. A hug was the only thing she could think of, so she pulled away from James, gave him a quick kiss on the cheek, walked over to Claire and wrapped her in her arms.

That was all Claire needed: comfort; an embrace. She relaxed, and hugged her back.

James hobbled over and joined the hug. Two of his girls.

"What is going on here? James, why are up? You should be off that leg and resting." His third girl said with a laugh as she walked through the doorway into the kitchen carrying two big bags.

"Hi Mom," both James and Claire said at once and both switched from hugging Maggie, to hugging their mom. Claire had recovered her wits sufficiently to be able to act completely normal for her mom, who was ramrod accurate at sensing if something was wrong. She was off the hook for the moment because she noticed that her mom's curiosity had another focus. She had a few minutes at least.

Ann Culver stood back from her two children and smiled sweetly at Maggie, "Hello, my dear Maggie, does Claire have you working overtime? Will you be joining our little dinner? I hope I brought enough food."

"Mom, are you serious?" James started laughing. He knew his mom was fishing. "You always bring enough food for 80 people. Maggie doesn't eat *that* much."

Ann pointed at James threateningly, "YOU sit. Get off that leg."

'Yes, Ma'am," James complied obediently. He sat down in the chair closest to where Maggie was standing and grabbed her hand. "And, Maggie isn't on the clock. She's here as my guest...she's my girlfriend." He looked up at her adoringly and brought her hand to his lips.

Ann clapped her hands together, "Whoohoo! Really? It's about time, son." She went straight for Maggie and gave her a big mama bear hug while saying, "Welcome to the family."

"Mom, slow down," James reacted in mock horror. "She's my girlfriend, not my wife." Then he winked at her, "yet."

"You slow down, buddy." Claire joined the conversation. "Don't scare Mags away."

"Mom, how was your trip?" James changed the subject, and Ann began recounting the crazy details of her last trip.

Beaming, Maggie just took it all in. She felt so loved. Her own family was great but they lived so far away. It was nice to feel a part of a family beyond her work family. She had called her mom earlier as she sat in her office full of roses. James had gone to four different florists to get all those roses. She had taken three bouquets to her house, and brought one here. It was on the kitchen counter.

Maggie went back behind the counter and gathered up the vegetables she had been cutting for James to snack on, and put them in baggies in the fridge. Claire joined her while her mom talked about her recent adventure and doted on the injured.

"So, *James* got you all those beautiful *red* roses?" Claire asked Maggie.

"Yes." Maggie blushed again. "I was totally surprised. Well, maybe not totally, if I'm honest. We have been spending a lot of time together since his accident. I always just thought he was a flirt and a ladies' man. But he told me he's been interested in me for a while, he was just unsure." She looked at Claire. "I didn't flirt back."

"Of course you didn't," Claire agreed. "He was a 'player.' Or so you thought."

"Exactly," Maggie lowered her voice, "But I fell hard for him at your party two years ago."

"I knew it." Claire poked her shoulder. Claire was relieved to be talking and thinking about something other than how she was feeling about Andrew. She felt free again. "But I wasn't sure how he felt, or I would have told him to stop bringing dates to all our family events."

"That would have helped, probably." Maggie laughed. "Actually, if it hadn't been for…" She stopped herself from continuing that Andy had set her straight about James' playboy status.

"Been for…?" Claire asked.

She had to think fast, "…the… accident, and…and… me being there for him…to help him…last week."

Oh my gosh. please buy it, please buy it, Maggie begged. Her heart was racing now. How could she have been so careless?

"That can be a story for the grandchildren,

right?" Claire elbowed her in the ribs.

"Yeah."

Whew.

Chapter 41

"I can't believe this game system still works."
Andy remarked as he held a game controller in his
hands and stared at the TV screen intently. He
jerked his controller violently to the left, and then
up, and then down again.

"I can't believe I can still beat you. AHA!" James
raised his arms triumphantly as he made a move
that scored higher than Andy. They were sitting on
James' sofa alternating between Tony Hawk and
Super Mario, their college favorites. They were
currently "skating." It was something to do that
didn't involve James moving around. The doctor
had been upset with him at his checkup this
afternoon. He had been trying to move around too
much. James had been hoping he could get a
walking cast, but the doc said not for another week
at least.

"Are you sure you don't want to tell me about

the other dates?" James said after a little time.

"GAAAA!" Andy shook the controller in frustration and set it down on the coffee table with a dramatic flourish. "I'd better do something to stop you from outscoring me."

James laughed and set his controller down next to Andy's. He adjusted his position on the sofa so he could see Andy better.

"I should have taken notes or something. I don't think I can remember details from all of them." Andy scratched his head, stretched his arms over his head, leaned back against the cushions and left his hands resting on top of his head. "Where did I leave off?"

James thought for a moment, "I think the last one I heard about was the tour at the candy factory."

"Good grief, that was over a week ago."

"I don't think I've seen you since I told Maggie I was in love with her, and that was last Wednesday. Seven days, four hours, 45 minutes, and..." James looked at his watch.

"Well then. Sheesh. Let's see. After See's Candy, I went to the zoo with the first Jessica. She is the one we can actually call Jessica. And she's the only one I discovered that I can have a decent conversation with. She's the actress. Don't laugh."

Too late. James was laughing. "Are you both *acting* like you are having a conversation?" James kept laughing.

"Shut up." Andy shook his head and glared at

James. "ANYWAY. She was okay. She's a little clingy, like the other Jessica, the one we are supposed to call Renee. What is it about the name Jessica? ...such physical creatures." He shook his arms like he was trying to rid himself of them. "She was always grabbing my hand and pulling me this way and that; 'look over here, ooh, and look over here,' like she'd never seen an elephant before. I didn't get a chance to talk to Claire at all at the zoo. It has been my goal to have at least a short conversation with her each time I see her. Claire stayed in the golf cart while Jessica and I walked. So, I failed there." He took a drink of his soda and continued.

"The next day I had 2 dates. The first was in the morning for breakfast on the Santa Monica Pier. That was with...um...Linda?...no Lindsay. She is a sales rep of some kind. I don't remember. We ate and then walked around the pier. She had never been there before. She was from Newport Beach, so I was surprised she had never been, but I guess they have enough piers in the OC, so why drive all the way up to Santa Monica? Anyway...we rode the Ferris wheel and she got sick. So, when the crew was tending to her to help her feel better, I sat down on a bench with Claire and we talked. I asked her why she decided to be a director. We had a nice, easy conversation totally about her. I want her to know that I'm interested in knowing all about her. At one point she just looked at me funny. I could not read her expression. If I had to guess it was a mix between confusion and contentment."

"That was probably accurate." James offered. "I think you are doing fine. She needs lots of time, and consistency. You've started chipping away at her granite façade." He made like he was using a hammer to pound on a chisel.

"So then, that evening I met Parker. She is also the other Ashley. She decided to go by her last name." Andy smiled really wide. "She is *gorgeous*. Long, blonde, surfer-girl hair, big brown eyes, athletic ...the works. BUT... She's probably 20 years old. I don't think I'm comfortable with that large of an age gap. She talked nonstop about indie country bands that I had never heard of and was constantly sticking her earbuds into my ears to have me listen to them. Eww."

"Eww," James started laughing again as he tried to sing, "Young teacher, the subject, of schoolgirl fantasy..."

Andy laughed, too. He hadn't thought of that. They both sang, "Don't stand so...don't stand so...don't stand so close to me."

"Was *she* comfortable dating an old man?" James was still laughing.

"Again...Shut Up." Andy said seriously, but then smiled. "Apparently she was," and winked at James, who gave him a disgusted look.

"No, really, she was a winker." Andy winked again. "She would wink at me every now and then while she was talking: the whole night. It got weird after a while. Maybe she thought it was endearing. I did *not* think so." He paused and then asked, "Is this how the show is every time? Are the girls usually this nuts?"

"No." James answered quickly. "Unless Claire is a magician in editing, the girls are usually normal and attractive, and the fans love them. The guy has trouble choosing. This sounds totally foreign to me. In fact, if you hadn't just asked that, I would have asked *you* if *you* were making this all up."

"I'm certainly *not* making this up." Andy insisted. "I don't think it is possible to make all this up. Unless, you were writing a book about crazy dates, and had to make stuff up."

"Well, Parker and I went to a go-cart race track. You know, the place where you can race in those little race cars around and around an indoor track?" Andy grimaced. "She had indicated on her profile that she enjoyed car racing, and I'm not bad at it either, actually, as I discovered last week. The trouble came when we went to sign up and found out that her experience with car racing was watching NASCAR. Not driving. And when I say, not driving, I mean it. She doesn't have a driver's license."

James stared. "And you promise you're not making this up?"

Andy shook his head with raised eyebrows. "So, get this, the place would not make an exception, so Claire got some shots of her in full gear putting on the helmet, getting in the car, talking smack, getting out of the car, taking off the helmet and acting like she had just beat me on the track. She was a good little actress for that."

"Did I hear you say you drove?" James asked, "Did you just drive by yourself?"

Andy beamed, "This is the best part. Claire suited up in the same gear as Parker, put on the same helmet, and *raced me around the track three times*."

"NO WAY!" James almost stood up. "My *sister* got in a *race* car?"

"Oh Yeah!" Andy rolled his eyes in pleasure. "Your sister looks hot in that racing outfit."

"Now *you* shut up." James punched Andy in the shoulder.

"And when she climbed out of the car, and took her helmet off and shook out her hair..." Andy closed his eyes, remembering. "Hmmm...I'd looove to see that played back in slow motion."

James socked him again.

"She was so pumped with adrenaline that she ran at me laughing and screaming and almost jumped into my arms, and then stopped herself short and just gave me a high ten." Andy looked off into the distance. "It was epic."

"Okay." James got serious. This was his baby sister, after all, "Next date."

The doorbell rang.

Chapter 42

Andy got up to get the food they had ordered earlier and both men were now chowing on Chinese food.

When Andy had gotten his fill, he continued, "Saturday morning, I met the one named Chloe at her place of employment."

James raised his eyebrows as he continued to scoop fried rice into his mouth.

"She works at this animal sanctuary in Sylmar. Claire told me on the way to the place—we rode in the same car all the way there, by the way—that she had thought it was a perfect date, because I had mentioned in my interview that I liked animals. At the sanctuary I could get to know Chloe in her element and enjoy the animals at the same time. She is an animal activist and is 'totally into helping those animals that need help.'" He had used his girl voice to mimic what James assumed was a phrase that was repeated throughout the morning.

"I've never heard of this place," James said after swallowing his last bite. "What kind of animals did they have there?"

"Sloths."

"No WAY," James said excitedly.

"WAY." Andy answered back. "She is a sloth enthusiast, to say the least."

"Did you get to *hold a sloth*?" James was beside himself. What a cool thing.

Andy smiled, "Of course. Are you kidding? On a date with a sloth maniac? I could not have avoided it if I wanted to."

James sat up and leaned forward, "What was it like? Are they soft? Do they really move that slowly?"

"They were baby sloths, and yes, they move in slow motion." Andy mimicked how the sloths had moved in his arms. "They are soft and they make the funniest noises. Like a cross between a squeak and a grunt. Claire and I just laughed the whole time. My face hurt after so much smiling."

"Wait. You and Claire? What happened to Chloe?"

"She handed me a sloth, and then handed one to Claire, and then had to leave to take care of something in another part of the sanctuary. We all just looked at each other and shrugged. We thought she wasn't on the clock, but apparently her work is important so she was just stepping in to handle whatever it was because she happened to be there."

"That is dedication for you." James smirked. "Animals are more important than humans to some people."

"I just enjoyed being with Claire." Andy closed his eyes again, remembering. "It was fine with me.

"Two more," James snapped him out of his reverie, "Hop to it, dude, I think Maggie said she was going to try to stop by on her way home."

"How nice for you," Andy said sarcastically. "Okay, number nine, number nine, number nine... I think it was JessLynn. The third and final Jessica. She is in real estate; not an agent, but works for one. And she is also a massage therapist." He rubbed his hands together, "Bonus."

"You're funny."

"We went surfing on Sunday." Andy announced in monotone with a perfectly straight face.

"You don't surf."

"I know."

"What the heck?"

Andy shook his head, "I know. Just call me stupid. I went bonkers in the interview when Claire wasn't there and I was making stuff up, and talked about my surfing hobby. Did I never tell you I surfed the Wedge in Newport every weekend in high school?" He said in mock surprise.

"THAT. IS. HILARIOUS." James had been relaxing back into the cushions, but was now sitting back up on the edge of his seat.

"When I found out I was supposed to dress for

the beach on Sunday, I panicked. I suddenly remembered what I had said in the interview and put it together that Claire was planning dates that had everything to do with my interview answers. I got in touch with Maggie and she told me not to tell anyone that she told me, but that I might be teaching this girl to surf."

James was smiling widely and loving every minute of this.

"So, I had to think fast. I showed up to pick her up with my arm in a sling. I made up some story that I had strained a muscle in my shoulder lifting weights and that I was immobilizing it to help it heal."

"You don't lift weights."

"I know."

James was having a hard time keeping it together.

"I couldn't try surfing *for the first time*, while pretending to teach some girl how to do it, *on camera*." Andy started laughing along with James.

Andy then added semi-seriously, "That was when the massage therapist thing came in handy."

"Oh NO," James was laughing even harder now.

"No really," Andy still trying not to laugh, "She insisted. And she was expertly thorough. This shoulder was sore from the massage for two days." He rubbed his left shoulder gingerly.

"So did you make it to the beach?" James asked.

"Oh yes, that was where my 'injury' worked in

my favor even further. It turns out that JessLynn actually surfs, so she had a wet suit, and a board. We did some 'action' shots on the shore where she did most of the actions, and then she ran out into the waves and surfed for about 30 minutes. They got some shots of her surfing, while I sat on the beach with your sister and talked some more. It was a beautiful morning."

"Did you save the best for last?" James sat back against the cushions, "I don't think I can stand any more excitement."

"Sunday night was very entertaining," Andy said after taking a few deep breaths and making sure that James had calmed down sufficiently. "Sunday night was the unforgettable Emma."

James raised his eyebrows. "Unforgettable?"

Andy continued. "Emma is a hairdresser like the very first girl, and appeared completely normal when I picked her up."

"What about your shoulder injury?

"I took my arm out of the sling, but I pretended to favor it all evening, which wasn't hard because it was so sore from the massage," Andy rubbed his shoulder again. "We went to see the laser show at the observatory."

"And this was unforgettable because?"

"Emma spoke in movie quotes all night."

"You're kidding." James cocked his head to one side and furrowed his brow.

"And if I didn't get the reference right away, she let me know immediately what movie it was from." Andy rested his head in one hand and looked at James with a, you-don't-even-know, look. "She told me it was a thing her friends dared her to do, and not to hold it against her."

"Did you try to quote back?" James asked, "You know, keep up? Take the challenge?"

"I thought about it...briefly...very briefly. I think I was able to come up with about three quotes," Andy admitted. "After a while I just stood back in wonder."

"She was that good?"

"The unforgettable Emma," Andy got up and stretched, "It really was impressive, but it got annoying. I finally had to try to anticipate what she was going to say to combat the urge to run, you know, make it a contest of sorts."

He walked over to the front window and looked out. "Maggie just pulled up, so I will go. She may have more to say. Claire told me that Maggie was editing all of it this week. I guess the first show airs on Saturday night."

Chapter 43

Claire sat down in front of the TV with her bowl of ice-cream. What a crazy week. After shooting the last of the dates, she had spent the beginning of this week going over footage of the first four dates with Bill to create the third episode. The first and second interview episodes were ready. The world would meet Andrew and the ten girls in two-hour specials spread over the next two Saturday nights, and then each week they would air three of the dates.

She was tired. They were ahead of schedule. Maybe she would just sleep in tomorrow and take the day off. They had all been working every day for the last two weeks. Yes.

She typed a text to Maggie and hit send. Maggie would relay the message to the rest of the crew to take a three-day weekend. They would be glad, and grateful. She was a good boss. They worked hard, and they always knew they were appreciated.

She dozed in front of the TV and found herself in a pretty meadow of flowers walking hand in hand with someone. She felt peace and contentment. She felt loved and secure. When she looked at her companion, she couldn't see his face, but she knew she loved him, and he loved her.

She woke with a start as her TV was all of a sudden louder than it was before. And there was Andrew smiling at her on the screen. They were playing the promo for the cycle opener. He looked right at her and said, "I'm looking for you, my love." Butterflies erupted in the pit of her stomach. It was as if he was talking to her, and she found herself wishing it was true.

She had to admit he was growing more and more attractive each time she saw him. He was so easy to talk to, and fun to be with. She found that she looked forward to the dates because she knew she would see him and he would try to talk to her.

They had sat on a bench on the pier last Friday morning and talked for at least 45 minutes while Lindsay recovered from motion sickness. He had asked endless questions about her family and her high school and college experiences. They talked about UCLA and she didn't think she recognized until just then that he had been there just before her. That was remarkable. She should have asked him if he ever knew James, but she didn't think of it at the time. He just made it so easy to talk about herself. He was interested. He would look at her with genuine interest. She remembered thinking that very thing when she first met him. Just sitting and talking was comfortable. It was a beautiful morning.

That evening, Andrew met Parker—the other Ashley. When Andrew picked her up and walked her to the car, Claire almost stopped the whole thing. This girl looked like she was still in high school, and Claire had to look at her file just to be sure she was of age. She had not looked this young at that initial meeting when they decided what to do about the same-name thing. The file said she was 22 years old. That was pushing it. She would have to speak to Ethan later. The girl was stunning, though. She would look good on camera. And she seemed normal enough, until they found out she didn't drive and the date was at a race car track. Another thing to speak to Ethan about. Claire had done some quick thinking, but it resulted in having to dress up in the same gear as Parker and actually get into one of those cars herself. She had to talk herself into it in the bathroom while she was changing. She had never done it before and did not want to make a fool of herself in front of her crew, and, if she was honest, in front of Andrew. The outfit was skin tight and leather with flattering racing stripes down the sides of her legs.

When she emerged from the bathroom and approached the group, she thought she heard a low whistle, but couldn't be sure who had done it.

It could have been Sid or Mark, or even Terry being supportive, but she secretly hoped it had been Andrew. She directed Parker to do all the things she would be doing if she were going to drive. She put on a great show of putting on the helmet and getting in the car, and shouting predictions of her success. Then Claire had gotten in the car and raced around the track. During the third time around, she passed Andrew. She had just been trying not to crash, but had slowly caught up to him and then was able to overtake him on one of the turns. What a rush. She found herself enjoying the thrill of the turns and the speed, and especially knowing she beat him to the finish. It was such a rush that she almost jumped into his arms at the end. She caught herself just in time. That would have been even more awkward than the baseball game.

Saturday afternoon they had to drive for almost an hour to get to the sloth sanctuary. The conversation she had with Andrew in the car was hysterical. They laughed and laughed. She was having too much fun to notice that Mark and Terry were strangely silent in the front seat the whole time. He taught her the game called "Would You Rather." She had never heard of it, but apparently it was all the rage at parties. Parties she usually avoided. They took turns thinking of a choice to stump the other. Her favorite was "would you rather have a constant drool, or a constant runny nose?" Just imagining both of those situations made her laugh until her sides hurt. At one point they were laughing so hard she had grabbed his forearm and leaned into him for extra support. When she realized what she was doing she sat back up and looked at him. He had stopped laughing but was still smiling. It was a different smile than the laughing smile. His eyes had twinkled at her in adoration. At least that was what it felt like at the time. She could talk herself out of it pretty quickly. Of course he was smiling. They were just laughing after all.

At the sloth sanctuary, they were together again for a significant time, this time while holding the cutest animals on the planet. He had remarked that his face was starting to hurt from smiling so much. His date, Chloe, worked at the sanctuary and had to shorten the date at the last minute because of some sloth emergency, so they almost didn't go to the restaurant where they had reservations. Andrew talked them into it. "We deserve a good meal, don't we?" he had said. "We are not going to get fast food and then drive an hour." So, the four of them went to eat at the four-star restaurant. She had been seated right next to Andrew in the booth, and their legs would touch every now and then, sending an electric current throughout her body. Their hands touched when she put her napkin in her lap and then put her hands on the seat so she could adjust her position a little. She discovered that his hand was there, too. She didn't dare look at him then. She had let her hand linger there next to his for as long as she dared. He didn't move his either.

She could not figure out why she was letting herself do things like that. She had no right to be acting like this. He was under her direction on a dating show that would find him the love of his life. And *it couldn't be her*, for crying out loud. But she was so enjoying being with him. It was getting harder and harder not to both enjoy it, and be mad about it. If anyone ever said it was impossible to be happy and upset at the same time, they needed to experience her life right now.

She was also still confused as to why the girls the computer spit out were so completely wrong for him. Did he have some flaw she wasn't seeing? That thought would nag at her every now and then, but didn't seem to interfere with her ability to be completely attracted to him. It was like her subconscious was convinced the computers were wrong and that those results should not influence her feelings.

On the way back into the city from dinner, she had fallen asleep in the back seat, and though she would have sworn she had started out leaning against the door, she had awakened with her head on Andrew's shoulder. Comfortable, but horrified; she moved away slowly to see that he was also asleep with his head straight back on the head rest. She had no way of knowing if he knew she had been snuggled up to him like that. He smelled good so close to her in the car. She could smell him on her clothes when she got home. They smelled divine.

The next day he was supposed to go surfing with the massage therapist. They were both accomplished surfers, so Claire thought it was a perfect date. When they had arrived at the beach, she noticed Andrew's arm was in a sling. Her first thought was "when?" When could he have possibly hurt himself? They had returned late the night before, and it was only 8am. Had he gone to the gym early that morning? It was the only explanation, and it was certainly plausible, but something nagged at her. The girl—she had been referring to them as "the girls," not by their names like she usually did—was a great surfer and they got some good film of them together near the water talking, and of her surfing.

While the girl was in the water, Claire and Andrew sat on a towel and talked. He asked her about her schedule. Was it tough? Did she have free time? What did she do with it? You know...those get-to-know-you questions. Was he fishing for information about her love life? No, she really didn't get that vibe. He just seemed like he really wanted to know. And it was the most natural thing to do, to just sit there and chat like old friends. She found herself telling him things...about her feelings, about what was important to her, things she hadn't even told her mom, or her close friends. Why was she doing that? As she shared, she even had conscious thoughts that she was saying too much, but he would just nod and agree and validate everything she said. He made it easy to keep going with no judgement, no inappropriate comments, and just complete acceptance. At one point she almost talked about Karl, but she stopped herself.

He had finally said, "I can't believe you are single," as they were standing up and shaking the sand out of the towel. JessLynn had come in from the water and she was going to shower off and then they were on their way to brunch on the pier. His remark startled her, not because he had said it in the first place, but because she almost didn't hear it. He had said it so quietly to himself that she was surprised she had heard it. He hadn't said it for her to hear.

Sunday evening was the observatory with the last girl, Emma. She kept her distance this time. The girl was cute and everything she said got a reaction from Andrew, either a laugh or a surprised look. He must like her, she thought. Well, at least there are a couple of the girls that will work going forward.

Chapter 44

"She has no idea." Sid said when he brought his film in to Bill for editing.

"Are you sure?"

Sid nodded, "I think if she had an idea that we were rolling on *her*, she would have said something, and stopped it. She just trusts us way too much," he shook his head. "You would think she knew us better than that. Either that or she figures she's going to trash all the extra in here."

"Are there certain times I should look for?" Bill wanted to save time. "Mark and Terry gave me approximate minute marks. Terry has even started holding her hand in front of the camera for a few seconds to mark where the Claire scenes start so I can spot them easier on fast forward."

"Dang, I'm sorry, I'm not that creative," Sid hung his head, "Or thoughtful...I'll do better from now on."

"Thanks."

"Did the others get beach footage?" Sid asked. He had been filming the surfer girl the whole time, and was hoping one of the others had been getting the conversation he had heard from Claire and Andy as they sat on the towel.

"I have some of that from both Mark and Terry, while one focused on the girl in the water, the other was on Claire. They traded off."

"Oh, good," Sid was relieved. "Was there audio? Cause you'll get full audio from my camera."

"Actually, not much. I have been worried, so it is good that you got the audio. We will be able to use constant audio from your camera and video from both of their cameras. The only thing that isn't ideal is that in order to not be conspicuous, both cameras are behind Claire the whole time. You only see their backs and body language, and sometimes their faces when they turn to look at each other."

"I could hear some pretty personal stuff coming from Claire since I was standing in front of them," Sid admitted, "So I hope we aren't' going to use that."

"Heck no!" Bill shook his head, "Claire would have to sign off on any of this if it gets that far."

Chapter 45

"Did you tell Andy about Sam?" Maggie was snuggled next to James on the sofa. She had dropped by to spend some time and then got the text from Claire that they were taking a long weekend. That was fine for the rest of the crew, but she and Bill were going to use Friday to do some editing on the Claire/Andy footage, so she would just have a normal weekend. It would be nice to have Claire out of the studio for that.

"What about him"

Sam was the voice-over/commentator for the show. He was the "talent" as they called it in the business: the voice; the host; the face of Single No More. He was the only on-camera person on this reality show that was a professional. He was also crazy.

"Did you *warn* him?"

"What am I warning him about?" this was

getting interesting, James thought.

"Has Claire never told you about him?"

"Apparently not," James sat up a little without disturbing Maggie. Having her in his arms like this was becoming his favorite pastime.

Maggie was surprised. Sam was one of Claire's *favorite* things about the show. "He is the host." She sat up to face James to his profound disappointment. "He does the narration and some of the interviews. You have *seen* the show, right? I'm surprised Claire hasn't told you about him."

"Oh, him," James remembered. "I don't think I ever paid attention to his name." He tried to coax Maggie back in his embrace. She willingly complied. It was her favorite pastime, too. "I guess you'll have to fill me in since my sister has decided I'm not worthy of her narrative."

"Sam is a character. He likes to be the center of attention, and sometimes he goes too far." Maggie started giggling. "Claire loves him, but can't stand him at the same time. It all depends on his mood and hers."

"Why are you laughing?"

"Well, there was this one time, we were getting ready to film interviews with the final two girls," she was still giggling. "All of production was ready and we couldn't find Sam. It was a really hot day. We were all standing around sweating because we had decided to film on the balcony of the villa because the clouds were amazing and it was going to be a great background, but the clouds made it a little more humid than we anticipated." She stopped to giggle some more.

"And..."

"There was a big splash below in the pool area and, well, we were all really sweating and a little irritable at this point. Claire got this look on her face and said to everyone, 'If he just jumped in the pool, I'm going to kill him, and then I'm going to fire him.'"

"What an idiot!" James started laughing too. "It was him, right?"

"Yep." Maggie nodded. "Claire sent one of the interns downstairs to tell him to just go home and that she was shooting the interviews herself. He was fully clothed, floating on a blow-up toy in the deep end, screaming at someone to bring him a drink."

"Piece of work."

"Claire doesn't put up with it, and so he doesn't get half the pay he would get if he behaved. It's just tough on her because she has to improvise." Maggie continued, "The fans love him, though, so she keeps renewing him each cycle."

"So why do I need to tell Andy about him?"

"He has an uncanny knack for discovering things," Maggie sat up again and adjusted her snuggle position. "He is the one who usually finds out things about the show contestants that no one else knows."

"And you waited until now to tell me this?" James was scratching his head.

"I thought you knew about him." Maggie apologized. "If there is something between Andy and Claire, Sam will spot it in seconds and expose it to the world, or at least to everyone within earshot."

"Couldn't you intervene?" James was hopeful.

"If I know Sam, he wouldn't be able to hold it in or be discreet," Maggie was adamant, "He's crazy, and unpredictable."

"It sounds like Claire needs a new host."

"Don't we all know it."

Chapter 46

James said to be really careful around this guy, Andy thought as he shook hands with Sam. "Nice to meet you, too," He apparently has a nose for news. It sounded like he should be a reporter, not a reality show host.

They were all together for the first time. Well, all the ones who were left, anyway. He had informed Claire that he would not need any more dates with Ashley, Brittany, Parker, Chloe, or Emma. He wanted to give them all the boot, but that would probably set the show back and they might decide to cut him loose. He couldn't risk that.

She was confused about Emma, "But you were so engaged in her conversation," she wondered about it out loud.

"Did you happen to hear any of it?" He started laughing softly as he shook his head and rolled his eyes.

"No, I wasn't close enough that night." She was looking up at him curiously. He was still laughing to himself.

"Everything out of her mouth was a movie quote." He smiled without showing his teeth or using his eyes.

"Oh NO!" she covered her open mouth with her hand.

"Yes."

She must not be editing any of it yet, or she would know this, he thought. He didn't know that she hadn't been in to editing at all. She couldn't do it. She couldn't watch him with the other women.

So here he sat in a room full of people. It was a bit chaotic, and he had to fight the urge to just watch Claire in action. He didn't want Sam to "notice" anything. Now he was paranoid.

Lissette, Lindsay, and all three Jessicas—go figure—were there. He had taken to calling them the Ls and the Js in his mind, just to keep it from exploding. But he was going to have to remember which was which or he would look bad. The girls were all sitting on chairs opposite his on the interview set. Sam was in the middle.

He became aware that Claire was giving instructions to all of them and thought he had better listen.

"Okay, folks, we are going to start rolling, and Sam is going to ask questions. Just answer them like you are sitting in your living room chatting with your best friends. Ladies, please wait until you are introduced. We will take one date at a time, so you will know when it is your turn. Forget we are even here."

Claire stuck her finger in the air and made circles to signal the cameras to start rolling. The intern walked in front of all the cameras one at a time, said something, and closed the clapperboard.

The group interview could have turned into something from the Jerry Springer archives, but it was a classy show, and everyone knew to be respectful and even tempered. Andy couldn't imagine the girls going crazy on him. Everything about his promo and his interview was the opposite of crazy. The women had to know if they wanted anything to do with him, they would leave the drama at home.

Sam started out asking Andy to describe his dates one at a time. Andy was careful to describe the ladies in a good light, adding little hints here and there about things that he liked about each girl. He had done a lot of prep work with Maggie for this, so he remembered names and facts correctly. She reminded him that he could mess up, and they would fix it later in editing.

He mentioned all ten dates in chronological order briefly, and then went into more detail about the five remaining ladies starting with Lissette, and finishing with JessLynn. When this episode aired, the audience would have seen all ten initial dates, but this was the reveal of the five eliminations. The fans would know by the end of the interview which ladies remained on the show.

Lissette had decided not to wear all black on camera. Either Missy, from wardrobe, had counseled her, or she had come up with it on her own. She had on black leggings and a big grey sweater. Still monochromatic; but not as depressing. She looked nice, and spoke up sufficiently. Sam's manner must have helped her shyness.

Sam was actually pretty good at putting his subjects at ease, but Andy was nervous about his supposed unpredictability.

He was thinking this exact thing when Sam asked with a smirk, "So, tell us, Andrew, who in this room do you *really* like best?" They had finished with the details about the remaining five ladies, so the reveal was complete.

The question threw him just a little, because he couldn't tell if this was something Sam did to everyone, or if he had already figured it out. He had said, "in the *room*" for heck's sake, and Claire was in the room. It was amazing how paranoid you could get when you were trying to hide something. Everything you do seems so transparent to you, that you end up tripping yourself up. Come on, actor, he said to himself, start acting.

"Now, Sam, if I answered that question, we wouldn't have a show, would we?" He smiled slowly into Camera 2.

He's good, thought Terry as she operated

Camera 2. Keep it up, Romeo; they'll be eating out of your hand. Every girl watching this will want you. They had started getting letters just from the promos before the first episode even aired.

Sam chuckled and looked over at the ladies, "Well, girls, you have your work cut out for you."

"Cut. Nice work everyone." Claire stood up and signaled her camera operators to stop with her hand circling the air. She was done with this. It was making her sick. She usually had them keep rolling, but she wasn't in the mood. She needed to get out of there, but she and Maggie still had to conference with Andrew about the next dates.

Mark ignored her signal and casually aimed the camera at Claire by cradling it in the crook of his arm like he was just holding it. He had been practicing this technique and had it perfected.

Sam ran around flirting with all the ladies in the room, including Andy's "ladies." He was notorious, but harmless at the same time. He was easy to flirt with because he was not a threat.

Andy noticed this and made a mental note to use this in his favor in the future. He made his way over to Claire. She had told him before that they needed to speak about the next dates before he left. When he got closer, he noticed that something was wrong. She was visibly bothered by something, and he hoped it wasn't him. It clouded his expression.

Claire saw Andrew approaching her like she told him to, so she motioned to him and mouthed that he should go to Maggie's office in five minutes. She was fully prepared to make Maggie do the arranging. She couldn't face him right now.

Maggie was on the other side of the set, but she saw the whole thing. *Her* office? *What*? Oh no, Claire, you are not getting out of this, she thought to herself, you have been avoiding anything relating to him for a whole week. It stops today. Maggie backed out of the room before Claire could catch her eye and give her the assignment. She ran down the hall and ducked into the editing studio. Her phone buzzed with a message from Claire that said, "meet me in your office." She didn't reply. Claire will have to go there now herself because she won't let Andy be stood up.

"This is nuts," Maggie said out loud to no one.

Chapter 47

Andy waited in front of Maggie's office for about seven minutes before Claire came around the corner. He was relieved to see her. She looked upset and annoyed.

"I can't find Maggie and she's not answering my texts." She brushed past him and indicated to him to follow her. She unlocked her own office and invited him to enter.

"Are you okay?" Andy was sincerely worried. "You look like you either don't feel well, or you are angry and trying to hide it."

"Wow," she looked right at him and visibly relaxed. How does he do that? They were now completely alone in her office. "You totally nailed it. How did you do that?"

He took a small chance, "I feel like I've gotten to know you pretty well over the past few weeks; especially your facial expressions." Her expression softened and she didn't object to that comment so he continued, "who are you mad at?"

She laughed, "Honestly? ...myself."

He feigned horror, "What did you do?"

"It's nothing to concern you," she smiled hoping to distract him from continuing his questions. "We need to discuss your next dates. We only need to plan one date, and then you take each one of the women on the same date, so you can see how each woman acts in the same situation. I have found it helps you get a perspective when you see how each one of them reacts to the same stimulus."

"That is actually brilliant," He was intrigued and suddenly had an even more brilliant idea.

Claire continued, "So what would you like to do for the date activity? Think of something you enjoy doing, and would be interested to see how each of the ladies responds."

"Well, I actually have an idea of something I'd like to try, but I don't want my first time doing it to be on one of the dates. You know, in case I freak out."

Claire looked confused, "you want to do something you've never done before?"

Andy took a deep breath. Here goes, "I want to try ziplining. I mean, I'm not a daredevil or anything, but I have always been curious. I think it would be a great activity to see what the women can handle. And what they are willing to do. There's a fear factor, and I am curious to see how each one of them react, but want to do it first by myself so if I pee *my* pants, I don't pee my pants on *camera*." That all came out in one breath.

"I agree with that," Claire nodded, "that is reasonable. So go do it, and then let me know what you decide. Can you go tomorrow?"

"Will you come with me?" there, he said it.

"What?" she sucked in her breath, "ME?" Her heart started beating fast. Is he playing with me? He is playing with me. He is totally playing with me.

"I know I said I wanted to do it first by myself, but I didn't mean *by myself*, just not with one of *them*." He said pointing in the direction of the studio.

But he thought, *I want to do it with you. I want to be alone with you. I want it to just be you and me with no camera crew*. As he looked at her, he willed her to somehow hear what he was thinking.

She stared at him. He had called the ladies, *"them"* which sounded both frightfully impersonal, and wonderfully encouraging to her. If he had done that on purpose, she noticed. But she still couldn't decide what he meant by what he was asking. What was his motive? Did he want to be with her, or did he just need a companion to test out his activity plan? She knew she couldn't come out and ask. That would put her heart in jeopardy. That would be taking a chance that she just wasn't willing to take. She was close, but still deathly afraid.

The thought of being totally alone with him was

delicious and irresistible, so she went with her heart. What the heck, "I've never done it, myself, but I've always been curious. It looks really fun...so...sure, let's go test it out for you."

"No cameras."

"No cameras."

They got on her computer and made reservations at place in the mountains east of L.A.

Chapter 48

He picked her up the next morning. Claire answered the door in jeans and a rock concert t-shirt. She was smiling and looked totally stress free. She looked fantastic. It was all he could do not to pull her into his arms and kiss her right then. Patience.

He had told James what they were doing and swore him to secrecy. He almost didn't say anything at all, but thought he had better at least have James on his side to run interference in case Maggie was looking for Claire for some reason. He wanted her all to himself. Claire had messaged Maggie the night before and told her she was staying home the next day because she wasn't feeling well. Claire had giggled and admitted to Andrew that she felt like a teenager ditching school.

They talked like best friends all the way up the mountain. She knew all about him already, so the conversation was mostly about her. She had never been with a man who was so easy to talk to.

"Is your family going to come out from Indiana for the finale? Or are they leaving you on your own for this adventure," Claire asked as they pulled up to the resort with the zipline.

"My parents think I'm nuts for doing this," Andy answered, "So I doubt they will make an appearance, unless I can convince them that I've found the love of my life." He lied. He had not even told his parents about this whole thing. No one in his family watched the show that he knew of. If things worked out the way he was hoping, he wouldn't need to. He decided to be honest about one thing, "They are coming out to take my nieces to Disneyland in June anyway. I'll see them then."

"How old are they again?" Claire got out of the car and put her little backpack on. She had brought a backpack instead of a purse.

"12 and 7." Andy was disappointed that she hadn't let him open the car door for her. Keep it casual and not like a real "date," he had to tell himself. "Neither of them has been to Disneyland, so my sister says it's all they have been talking about since Christmas."

"I'm surprised that you haven't offered to take them before now." She fell in step with him as they approached the zipline office. "I mean, really, that's a long time for a favorite uncle to live near the happiest place on earth and not host a trip there."

He laughed and nodded, "Yes, well, my sister didn't want to spoil them. I have offered many times since I moved back. She wanted them both to be at least old enough to remember their experience and appreciate it."

"That is pretty smart."

"She still thinks Avery is too young, but Alexa is just the right age to still be in awe, and to appreciate it at the same time."

"Are you going with them?"

"Maybe. It depends on my work schedule"

They signed all the waivers and sat through the safety instructions, strapped on their harnesses, and followed the rest of the group over to the chair lift that would take them to the first line. This place was normally a ski resort, and had capitalized on the zipline craze to generate income in the off season: a perfect pairing. There were 5 lines that connected from the very top of the mountain through a series of trails and other lifts and ended with a longer line that traversed the width of the resort to the bottom.

It was heaven being this close and this alone on the chair lift. Andy almost told her everything. He was so torn. He had no way of knowing if she shared his feelings or if she was just being nice. His instinct told him she liked him back. But was that enough to risk it right now? Probably not. James had said to go slow, and Andy thought he was moving even slower than a snail's pace.

It was a beautiful day. They could see for miles, which wasn't always the case in the Southland. It had been windy, so the haze was gone.

They got to the first line. It was a baby one: only about 20 feet, so that newbies could get a feel for it without too much anxiety. They had to climb up a ladder into a tree where the launch platform was. Andy went up first and held out his hand to help Claire with the last step onto the platform.

She grabbed his hand and pulled herself up next to him and then let go and grabbed onto his arm with both hands and looked up at him, "I don't know about this." She looked nervous.

"I know... me too," He agreed. They hung onto each other as they waited their turn.

***

"Are you getting this?" Mark asked Terry, "You are closer."

"I wouldn't say *closer* by any means, but I have a better angle than you. This would be so much easier if we didn't have to hide." Terry adjusted her earbud. Mark's voice was cutting in and out. They were too far away from each other for perfect reception.

"It's just too bad we can't get any audio," Mark whined, "I wanna hear what they are saying."

When James told Maggie about the zip line plan the night before, she almost didn't do anything. But then Terry had called her about something else, and Maggie let it slip that Andy and Claire were going rogue. Terry offered to take care of it, and called Mark and Sid. Sid couldn't make it, so she and Mark had called every zipline company they could find asking about "their" reservation for the next day, and finally discovered the one that Claire had booked.

They arrived at the resort about two hours before Andy and Claire and told the management basically what they needed to do without too many details, especially the names of the ones they were filming. They did not want anyone to alert Claire or Andy by accident.

Mark was in a tree at about the halfway point of the second line. There was no way he could be spotted unless his camera glinted off the sun by some miracle. Terry was nearer to the first platform on the ground under the cover of an outbuilding. After Claire and Andy were out of sight, she would jump on the lift back to the base and get into position to film their descent on the last line. Mark had an employee helping him. He was going to try to get out of the tree after they passed him, and ride an ATV down to a space near the 4th platform. The guy on the ATV was out of sight of the line, or at least not totally out of place. Mark didn't want any chance of alerting Claire to their presence.

This was the most exciting thing Mark had ever done. He loved his job, but this, right here, was exciting. Terry had agreed with him on the way up the mountain. They were good at being inconspicuous, but they never hid completely out of sight. Maybe they should start. People were less uptight and more natural when a camera wasn't shoved up their nose.

***

Claire went first. She clicked her harness onto the line and sat down just like they told her. She glided across to the other platform easy as pie. She exhaled as she stood up on the platform and the teenager who worked there helped her unhook from the line. She turned around and waved to Andy, "Whooohoooo. It's fun. It's not scary," She yelled.

She clapped her hands as he hooked on and glided over to her, and she threw her hands up as he unhooked and they shared a high ten.

Claire went first again. This one was longer. She hooted and hollered the whole way and never saw the camera in the tree about halfway down. Andy followed pretty quickly and came up to the platform really fast. He had forgotten to break like they told him to, so he almost slammed into the employee. They were used to this, so it was no big deal, but Andy was still apologetic.

"You take your life in your hands every day," Claire commented to the kid, who laughed it off.

Each line got longer and more exhilarating. Both Andy and Claire were loving every minute.

When they got to the 4th line, they discovered that it was two lines side by side. They could zip at the same time if they chose. "Let's do it," Claire decided. Andy was relieved and grateful that he didn't have to suggest it. The cute blonde employee helped them hook onto the lines and then said, "If you don't want to separate on the way down, you should hold hands."

Andy held out his hand and looked into her eyes. She smiled and put her hand in his and held on tight as they stepped off the platform at the same time.

By the time they hit the platform at the other end; Mark was already doing a happy dance as he packed up the camera and got on the back of the ATV to head to the bottom.

Chapter 49

Claire was still spinning from the day. She was sitting on her favorite chair in silence as she relived the experience. She didn't want any distractions from her memories. After she had held his hand on the penultimate zipline, she didn't want to let go. It felt too good; too right. The final line was long and had the best view of all, but it was lonely after sharing the previous one with Andy. When she landed and unhooked, she waited there and watched him descend toward her. She had taken off her helmet and was leaning on a support for the covering that shaded the landing pad.

Her hair was blowing around her face as she squinted up at him. He decided to spin around and flip upside down just for show. When he righted himself just before he hit the landing, she was laughing.

"You're crazy," she said through her laughter.

He unhooked and walked over to her and took off his helmet. He held out his arms for a hug. She didn't even hesitate; she walked right into his embrace and they held each other while he said, "Thank you for doing this with me. This is the most fun I've had in a long time," he paused and then pulled back so he could see her face, "with anyone." Then he hugged her again for a quick three seconds and let her go.

He grabbed her hand again as they walked back to the office where they returned their helmets and harnesses. She didn't want to let go, but she was conflicted. He was dating five other women right now on her reality show. This was highly irregular, but she didn't feel bad. She couldn't explain it.

As she sat in her chair. she tried to talk herself into believing that the only reason she was letting him get so close to her was because she knew there was no future there. He was safe. He was taken. She could let her heart flutter and feel the goosebumps without having to look into the future and see the hurt that would eventually rear its ugly head.

But wouldn't it be nice if it could be forever? She had never felt this comfortable with Karl, or with any of her boyfriends in college. It was like Andrew was a part of her, and had always been there. She could still smell him on her shirt from when they shared that hug.

On their way home they had talked about the

next zipline dates with the "fab five." She laughed right out loud when he called them that.

"You know, Andrew, you need to start thinking of them as individuals; instead of a collection."

He laughed back, "Please call me Andy, Claire. My best friends all call me Andy."

"Okay, Andy. Let's go over the date order. Who do you want to go first?"

"Uhhhhhh..." He looked bored and unwilling to answer.

"Andy," She put her hand on his arm and looked right at him. "You have to get serious here."

She found herself wanting him to say that he didn't want to go through with it anymore, and that he wanted her.

He looked back at her as he came to a stop at a light, and said softly, "Do I have to?"

Her heart had started beating wildly again as she looked into his eyes. Was he going to say why? He didn't look away until the light changed and the car behind them honked.

They drove for about 15 minutes in total silence. Then he said in monotone, "I guess we can go in ABC order."

Had he been waiting for her to say something? What was she supposed to say? All of his behavior was telling her that he was interested in her, not the other women. But he hadn't said anything. Why would he be paying her all this attention and not say anything about it? If he felt something for her, why was he keeping quiet about it?

She had another thought. Was he unhappy with his choices? Was that it? And if that was it, why hadn't he just said something? Those girls were computer matched to him. She was so confused and conflicted about that part of this whole situation; it made her unable to function.

In any case, she had this day to remember. She had felt happy and beautiful all day; all because of Andy. She just wished it could have lasted longer. She had almost asked him to stay for dinner, just to prolong the wonderfulness.

***

"I have just had the most wonderful day of my life," Andy said as he sat down on the chair opposite the sofa where James and Maggie were snuggled up together.

"Details, details," James prompted as he squeezed Maggie's hand to remind her not to say anything.

"Well, Claire and I went on a date."

"What?" Maggie feigned surprise. "A *date*? How did you pull *that* off?"

He leaned back in his chair and rehearsed the whole day for both of them, even the part about holding her hand. He also told them about the awkward conversation in the car. He wanted their perspective and advice. He was too close now to be objective.

Maggie spoke first. "I think that she is getting

close. If she let you hold her hand without objecting..."

"For sure, dude," James interrupted. "But I wonder if you are starting to confuse her even more. She's not stupid. She is probably trying to figure out why you are being so familiar and intimate with her, but not saying anything."

"I am just going on what you said about going slow." Andy sat up and lowered his head into his hands.

"If it wasn't for this dang show, you could just concentrate on her, but now you have to spend time with the "fab five," Maggie laughed, "I love that by the way."

"There's nothing fab about them." Andy said with his head still in his hands. "They are annoying now, because they are in my way."

Chapter 50

"Déjà vu," Terry mouthed and winked at Mark as they arrived at the resort. They were all on the mountain today. Because of the distance from the studio, Claire had decided to film all five dates in two days. They were all staying two nights in a hotel near the ski resort, so they wouldn't have to deal with traffic up and back twice. It was worth avoiding the headache. Plus, it was beautiful and the crew was excited for a sleepover. Andy was prepared with five changes of clothes so it would appear as though these dates were, in fact, on separate days. Two of the dates would include a breakfast, two would include a picnic on the mountain, and one would include dinner.

Terry had called ahead and made sure the entire staff knew not to mention to anyone that *any* of them had been there over the weekend. That included everyone in the party. She had no idea that Claire had called ahead about the same request. The manager had just laughed to herself. This was one crazy secretive TV crew.

Andy had had a full day before the trip to resign himself to the fact that he had to be nice and play along with getting to know these other women. He had to appear genuine even though it was eating him up inside. He also was fully aware that it was unfair to the "fab five." He wished there was a way to bring them into the whole charade. It would be easier on him if they knew about it and could be acting as well. He was pretty sure that at least a few of them would go along. He had gotten that much of a read on them during their first encounters. Jessica was an actress for crying out loud. She could do it. And the other two Jessicas, Renee and JessLynn, could probably pull it off. Lindsay had all but said she wasn't feeling it with him. She tried to assuage his guilt about making her so sick on the Ferris wheel, and had said it was okay if he didn't choose her. So that left Lissette. She was unreadable. The fact that she hardly spoke may work in his favor, but could she handle it without giving anything away?

And when would he ever have a chance to even talk to them all about it without a camera pointed at them?

He decided that he would wait until after the next elimination. Complicating the lives of three ladies was preferable to complicating the lives of five.

They filmed Andy and Jessica at the local diner for breakfast. It was a cute mom and pop diner with a lot of charm according to the crew. The couple seemed like they were enjoying each other. Claire sat in the van the whole time, only listening to the audio she was getting in her ear from the earbud system she shared with her camera operators. It was hard for her to see him and not go up and talk to him. He was turning into her best friend. He had asked her to call him Andy like his best friends do. Didn't that mean he considered her a best friend?

She was watching something on TV the night before that had cracked her up and her first thought was to tell Andy about it. Something a best friend would do. She had half of a text message written to him until she stopped herself.

When they got to the resort Terry got all harnessed up to be the close-up camera. She got to ride with them. Sid had not wanted to ride, and so she and Mark decided to alternate days. They drew straws in the diner for the first day which involved three trips down instead of two. Terry won. They had also attached helmet cams to each helmet so that they could work with that footage in editing.

It was weird being there again. There were so many wonderful memories. Claire had debated whether or not she should remain at the base, or go up the lift. The management was letting them use three of their ATVs, so she decided at the last minute to use one of them to follow the action. She thought it might be a fun distraction to ride one of them around all day, so at least she would enjoy something about the next two days.

She watched Terry get on the lift first and then Andy and Jessica followed on the next chair. Terry was able to turn and face them with her camera. The helmet cams were getting their audio. Sid and Mark filmed them for a few minutes until they got too far, then the three of them got on their ATVs and began the ascent up the mountain. They followed the chair lift for the most part and passed up Andy, Jessica, and Terry pretty quickly. They were able to get to the top about 10 minutes before them, and start setting up.

Claire was amazed that Sid and Mark were able to find vantage spots so quickly. They really are the best in the business, she thought. She rode with them to see where they would be and give her approval. She trusted them, but it was fun riding the ATV. She was getting the hang of how to maneuver it around. Sid parked himself right between the first two platforms, to film them on the short beginner line. Mark was halfway between the second and third platforms. They would have to hold up the riders so that the cameras could reposition after each ride. Terry would go before them to get their rides from head on. She had a lightweight camera that she could harness to her body while she rode the lines.

Claire could hear laughing coming from the lift. She looked over and Jessica was cracking up at something. They were almost to the top. Andy was laughing, too. Terry was getting off the lift so she probably hadn't caught it. Dang.

"That is the *funniest* thing I have ever *heard*. You should be a comedian." Jessica smacked Andy's shoulder and jumped off the lift a little too soon, but landed just fine, like an athlete. Andy looked panicked for a minute and then followed her off the lift a little less dangerously. Jessica ran all the way to the ladder at the bottom of the platform yelling, "Come ON, Andrew, let's do this, I can't wait to do this." Terry followed Jessica because she was infinitely more entertaining at this point.

Claire rode over to Andy and when she got close enough, he mouthed the words, "Whatever I said wasn't that funny." He shrugged his shoulders and smiled weakly. He trotted after Jessica.

After the first few zip lines, Mark's voice came through in Claire's ear. "This girl talks so loud. I am getting her audio through my camera and I'm at least 30 feet away most times. I hope she isn't peaking the speakers on the helmet cams. They aren't that sophisticated."

"Yeah, that wouldn't be ideal." Claire agreed, but wasn't sure how to fix it. They had never filmed on a zip line before. "We can't do anything about it now. Let's listen to a little bit at the motel tonight and see if it's okay. If we have to add some extra interview with her to make up for it, we can do that tomorrow."

"One of us could get the interview time with her today while the others are filming the picnic with JessLynn." Terry chimed in, "that way she's wearing the same clothes."

"What would I do without you guys," Claire blew them a kiss that they could hear rather than see. It's what she did to show them her love when they couldn't see her. She was actually having fun tooling around on this ATV. She had gotten the hang of reverse and was becoming adept at navigating the inclines. It was taking her mind off of what was going on over her head.

When they got to the tandem line, instead of grabbing her hand so they wouldn't get separated, Andy made the suggestion to link legs. Jessica thought this was a fantastic idea and after creating a leg tangle, she squealed the whole way. They even came apart about two-thirds of the way down and she didn't stop squealing. Andy took that opportunity of freedom to do his flip upside down. She thought that was also fantastic and gave him a standing ovation when he landed, and then jumped into his arms when he unhooked from the line. He was not expecting it, but recovered adequately enough to catch her without them both falling off the platform.

Claire was just getting to the platform and saw it all. She rolled her eyes. "We almost lost both of them just now. Terry, can you tell her to be careful, please."

"Yes, boss," Terry answered, and then they all

heard Terry politely tell Jessica to be careful.

"Good grief," Mark chimed in as he motored toward the base landing. "Hold them. I'm not ready yet."

Sid was already positioned just 20 feet down the line from the platform. He was also getting good at maneuvering his ATV.

They all heard Terry tell Andy to wait a few minutes until she got the go from Mark.

"Okay, babe," They all heard Jessica say, "This time I want you to go first, and I want you to catch me at the bottom." Andy's reply was inaudible.

"Babe?" Sid said with a laugh. Claire almost burst out laughing because she was thinking the same thing. "Second date, and she's calling him babe?"

Claire looked up at Terry, who had the camera in front of her face and was trying not to smile. Mark was laughing out loud in her ear.

Chapter 51

Andy was having a hard time with the fact that every moment was being recorded. He had to check himself before he spoke, which was making him nervous. When Jessica had jumped into his arms, his first reaction was to yell. She was fun, but a little too much for his taste. She was getting on his nerves. She called him "babe." Who does that? It was almost as though she was trying too hard for the cameras. As a struggling actress, she had that motivation. He could understand that, but it was still hard. He was trying. She kept touching him: holding his hand, grabbing his arm, she had even played with his hair on the chair lift. He wasn't used to a girl being so familiar so early in a relationship; especially in a relationship like this one.

JessLynn was next. They had prepared a picnic lunch for them at the top of the chair lift. He had gone back to the motel to drop Jessica off, change clothes and pick JessLynn up.

As soon as they sat down on the chair lift, JessLynn reached up and adjusted her helmet and then all of a sudden leaned close to him and in all seriousness asked in a whisper, "So do you like me?"

Caught off guard, he turned his head to face her and also whispered. "You know they are recording all of this."

She reached up as if to straighten his helmet but actually did something to the camera on the helmet. "They can't hear us now."

"Are you a tech wizard or something?" he laughed, "I've been trying to figure out how to shut those off just to have a moment of privacy."

"I turned mine off when we sat down. We have to continue being animated and hope they don't notice right away."

Andy was grateful and smiled, "To answer your question, I think you are a great person. You are attractive, and smart...and..."

"You're just not feeling it." she concluded." I can tell. I could tell on our first date on the beach." She didn't seem bothered. "I don't really feel a connection with you either, so don't feel bad. I mean, you are really cute, and super nice and polite, but there should be a spark, right?"

Andy nodded. What a windfall. Should he bring her in? She seemed intelligent and capable, and not psychotic. They were halfway up. He went for it. He took the next 4 minutes and told her all about why he was on the show.

"Oh my goodness, Andrew, what a story!" JessLynn was hooked. "I'm totally on board with this. What do you want me to do? This is so romantic."

"Really?" Andy couldn't have asked for a better result. "You won't give me away? You'll help?"

"This is the coolest thing I've ever done. I've got chills," It was like Christmas had come early, "This is what we are going to do. This is going to be so much fun," JessLynn quickly outlined a plan for their "relationship" so that she would remain on the show till the end or whenever Claire kicked her out.

To start it off, Andy put his arm around her and gave her a friendly side hug.

***

The picnic went off without a hitch. They acted normally. She even fed him some strawberries. It was convincing. They laughed and flirted the whole time on the ziplines. He gave her a genuine hug for the cameras at the end, mostly because he was grateful for a confidant and some company in his struggle. He dropped her off at the hotel, changed his clothes, and then picked up Lindsay.

JessLynn was going to feel out the other girls; just hint around to see how they felt about Andy and not say anything unless she felt sure about them. The last thing he needed was one of the girls running to Claire, or even to the network, to complain.

The ride up the lift with Lindsay was awkward. He figured that she had fully expected him to eliminate her after she got so sick, and was confused as to why she was still here. He spent the entire lift ride trying to figure out how to tell her it was okay, but ended up just making it worse because of the silence. He hadn't wanted to chance that her helmet cam was on. He had checked his and it was able to turn it off again.

So, he tried to be overly friendly, which wasn't natural for him.

"I don't think this girl is working." Mark mumbled as he was racing down the hill to get to the next vantage point.

"No?" Claire asked. She thought it was going great. Lindsay looked a little uncomfortable, but Andy was trying. And not making it. She had to admit it was easier to watch this date than the first two. It was refreshing to not have to watch another girl with her hands all over him. Jealous much? I guess it was time to admit she was jealous. If I'm feeling jealousy, then I've gone over the edge. She congratulated herself on finally being able to recognize and give a name to what she had been feeling. It's been jealousy this whole time; the anger and the confusion. It all fits. I've fought it for long enough. Now I have to let it go. Recognition is the first step in healing. I can call it for what it is and start letting it go. But could she let it go? Could she let him go? She was not so sure.

"Are you watching the same two people I am watching?" Mark laughed. Of course she was. This one wasn't as threatening as the other two. He got it. He just wanted her to get it.

"Well, they are a little stiff, but it's happened before." Claire tried to defend them.

No one was buying it as evidenced by the silence that followed in her ear.

***

Dinner with Lindsay was no less awkward. There was nothing he could say or do that made her relax. When the food arrived, he thought he would try the obvious. "You have been quiet all day and I get the feeling that you are uncomfortable. Do you want to talk about it?

She tilted her head and finished chewing on the bite of her hamburger. "To be completely honest, I expected you to eliminate me after what I said on the pier." She took a sip of water and continued, "I have been trying all day to figure out why you invited me on this adventure. I as much as told you flat out I wasn't attracted to you." She sat back and waited for his response.

Well, there was no coming back from that, for sure. "I'm sorry. I misread that whole thing. I thought you were just embarrassed that you got so dizzy on the Ferris wheel."

She laughed right out loud. "Dizzy. Wow. You're being a gallant gentleman for sure, I'm not sure I would call it being dizzy, but okay. You are very nice, but you don't have to invite me back. It was nice to meet you, but let's finish our meal, and I will get some sun at the pool tomorrow before we leave, and this can all be a memory. Good or bad." She took another bite of her hamburger.

He held up his soda, "To memories." They clinked glasses and smiled and enjoyed the rest of the meal.

"Well, there's honesty for you." Sid said.

"I like her," Claire added.

"Too bad she doesn't like him," Terry said smiling to herself. Of course Claire likes her.

"Well, it was a good, honest, heart-felt moment for the show, anyway. Cut. Let's pack up." Claire circled her finger in the air.

Chapter 52

After breakfast, Andy and Lissette got harnessed up for the zip line and sat through the class; his fifth lesson on ziplining. He could give the class himself now. Lissette had been extra animated during breakfast. Andy thought maybe she was less nervous about being around him now, or maybe she was pumped for the adventure. In any case, it was refreshing not to have to carry the conversation like he had on the previous date with her, and on the previous day with Lindsay. She was actually pretty cute when she smiled. He didn't remember her smiling at the aquarium.

When they got on the chair lift, she tucked her arm under his and grabbed onto it so tightly he thought she might be cutting off the circulation. She looked up at him and said softly, "Isn't it grand that it didn't rain today? That would have been a bummer." She winked at him with the eye that

Mark couldn't see from his spot on the chair in front of them.

His eyes got really wide and so did his smile. That was the signal that JessLynn told him to look for. If any of the girls said something about rain on the chair lift, that meant they were in the Andy-loves-Claire club. Yay, JessLynn. She really *was* into this.

Then Lissette surprised him even more. She winked again and said quite loudly, "I'm really not sure I want to do this. I'm really afraid of heights."

He grabbed her hand and squeezed it and pretended to earnestly talk her into it. He said all the normal things you say to someone to convince them to try something they are afraid of. She played along and fought it for most of the way up, and then became quiet and acted more nervous.

They got off the lift and walked slowly to the platform. It took them 15 minutes to talk her up the ladder, then another 25 minutes to get her to do the beginner zipline. She screamed bloody murder the whole 20 feet to the other side. It was all Andy could do not to laugh. She was an exceptional little actress.

The whole rest of the way down, she complained and whined, and fought. She was rude to the zipline operators; she would cling onto Andy for dear life and look longingly up at him. When they got to the tandem line, she insisted on holding onto his whole arm with both hands, which confused the employees because it really was more dangerous that way, and they had said as much.

Terry, Claire, and Sid were having a great conversation the whole time, which they usually did when they were filming a particularly difficult date. It usually turned into banter not unlike sports commentators.

"And here we go, folks, the banshee has left the station," Sid called just after Lissette launched from one of the early platforms, and her screams could be heard by everyone on the mountain. They were ear shattering and other-worldly.

"She should be taking a breath right...about...now." Terry would say just before the scream would stop momentarily.

Claire had never laughed so hard in her life.

Mark was prevented from making any comments unless he was alone on the platform waiting for Lissette and Andy to descend. Claire could tell it was killing him. He was usually the funniest.

"This has been *the* most entertaining two hours of my life." Mark finally said when he was at the bottom waiting for one of them to descend. "We have *got* to air this one first. I insist."

Claire was on her way down the hill and was almost to the bottom when she heard Mark's comment. She started laughing and then hit a bump that shifted her wheels parallel to the slope which was not ideal. She felt the ATV start to roll. She tried to turn the wheel downslope but it was too late. The last thing she remembered was

hearing someone scream her name from
somewhere over her head. It sounded like Andy.

Chapter 53

"CLAIRE!" Andy watched in horror as Claire's ATV jolted sideways and then rolled over her and continued down the hill. He could do nothing but scream her name as the zipline carried him past her and on down to the bottom.

Mark had heard Claire laughing, then she stopped abruptly, gasped, and then there was a thud, and then he saw Andy look down and scream Claire's name. He looked to where Andy was looking and saw the ATV rolling down the hill. He couldn't see Claire.

Mark shouted what was happening to alert Sid and Terry, and told the landing crew to alert the resort to send their emergency response team. He had taken off running up the hill toward Claire just as Andy landed.

Andy had gone before Lissette on this final line,

so when he got down, he unhooked his harness from the line and somehow got it off while frantically running back up the hill right behind Mark.

Terry got to her first. Claire had just passed Terry's position when she rolled, so Terry was closest.

Claire was lying unconscious on her back and there were bloody scratches on one of her arms. Terry knelt over her and listened for breathing, and tried to find her pulse.

Mark ran up yelling, "Don't touch her, she may have a spine injury."

"I know, Mark." Terry was calm. She could feel a pulse and Claire was breathing. "She is breathing."

Andy ran up next and knelt down next to Terry and gingerly took Claire's hand. "Claire?" The anguish in his voice was obvious to everyone. If they hadn't already known how he felt about her, they would have figured it out right then. This behavior only solidified their resolve to support him in his intentions for their boss.

Claire stirred and started to sit up, but then grabbed her head and laid back. Terry moved to cradle Claire's head in her lap.

"Wait, Claire," Andy said with obvious relief, "Don't move until we can see if you *should* move or not."

She opened her eyes to see Andy, Mark, and Terry looking down at her. "What happened?"

"You rolled your ATV, you kamikaze," Mark winked at her, "You trying to scare us to death?"

Sid rolled up and hopped off his ATV in a panic. "What the heck happened?"

"I think I'm okay," Claire sat up and checked her limbs, "My head hurts, but nothing else hurts apart from my elbow," She could feel a lump forming on the side of her head, "and my ego."

Andy looked at her arm and bent it out and in and tenderly felt for a break from her shoulder to her wrist. He never let go. Sid grabbed some wet wipes from his pack and handed them to Andy, and Andy gently wiped the blood from Claire's arm.

The emergency crew appeared with a basket to take her down the mountain. They checked her for obvious injuries, even though she was insisting there was nothing wrong with her.

She got up on her own and, sandwiched protectively between Mark and Andy, she walked down to the landing area. Lissette was waiting there in a panic, and Claire assured her that all was well. They would continue everything as planned.

"Okay, quit the China doll treatment, guys, I just need Ibuprofen and I will be fine. We still need to shoot one more date."

The resort medic came over and made her sit down and put an ice pack on her head and arm to combat the swelling. He did a concussion exam and declared that she was probably fine, but should be watched. "Don't let her sleep for the next 12 hours."

"You've *got* to be kidding?" Claire complained. She was beside herself. Of all the...

Mark smiled sweetly at Andy, "Okay, Sport, you need to go get your next date. There's a picnic waiting for you at the top." He gave no indication that he had witnessed any sign of tenderness or anguish on Andy's part when they were all kneeling over Claire. Andy thought he had been totally transparent.

Sid clapped Andy on the back, and half pushed him toward the parking lot. "Let's go, Romeo, you've got another Juliet waiting to be wooed."

Andy was confused. He was expecting weird looks and questions. But he was getting none of either. He looked over at Terry; certainly, *she* had noticed. She was smiling at him. He thought he saw a little of what he was looking for, but it didn't last long. Her expression changed suddenly, "Go get her, Cowboy," she said with a wink.

Go get HER, he thought? Did she mean Renee or Claire? And they had never called him names before: Romeo, Sport, Cowboy....

What the devil was going on?

Chapter 54

"I. AM. FINE." Claire declared through clenched teeth. She was frankly sick of being treated like a crystal vase. Mark and Sid were trying to talk her out of getting back on an ATV to follow the next shoot.

"Look, boss, you have already trashed *one* of their vehicles," Mark said with a wink.

"Shut *up,* and I mean it."

"Okay then, but you should know something," Mark said quietly. He got closer to her so that only she and Sid could hear him. "Andrew yelled your name as soon as you crashed. He had been floating over you at the time, and he never stopped yelling until he landed. Then, even though I had a pretty big head start, he almost beat me up the hill to where you were."

"He looked pretty torn up when I got there, too." Sid added seriously.

Claire stared at both of them. They were both waiting for a reaction. She frantically tried to formulate one that would make sense. "What? Really? How sweet of him. He is a really nice guy, isn't he?" She said this as innocently as she could.

They still looked like they wanted more than that from her. She wasn't going to give it. She got on the ATV and started up the hill.

Mark and Sid gave each other a look.

"That was weak and unconvincing." Sid said with a smile.

Mark nodded. "She's caving."

***

Claire tried to wrap her head around what had just happened. So now her camera crew had witnessed some interesting behavior on Andy's part when she was hurt. That wasn't as revealing as the actual news that he had reacted so strongly to her getting hurt. That very fact made her heart flutter just a little. He yelled her name and ran to her? She vaguely remembered hearing her name. Was that Andy?

She had to stop and think for a minute. She was about halfway up, and she was on a part of the trail that was out of sight of the chair lift. She got off the ATV and walked a bit until she was under a big pine tree. She sat down and tears began to roll down her cheeks. All the stress that had been building for the last two days, the accident and the conversations, came spilling out. She tried to cry without making any noise because only Adam could turn off the earpiece transmitters. It felt good to get all the emotion out.

She was overwhelmed that he had acted that way when he knew she was hurt. The realization that someone other than her family actually cared about her welfare was touching. Correction, the realization that a man that she was discovering she had feelings for also appeared to share those feelings, was touching and heart stopping at the same time. At least that was what she thought she could reasonably glean from his behavior.

He really ran all the way up?

She sat under the tree until she was able to calm her heart and her tears. Still unable to decide what to do about it, she got up and walked back to the ATV.

"Claire, are you alright?" She heard Sid's voice in her ear. How long was I sitting there? She thought.

"I'm fine, how are you?" She snapped back.

"Sorry, boss," he apologized, "We are ready to roll. Just wondering where you were. You can't disappear on one of those things now. We would have to call out the dogs."

"Keep your shirts on. I just stopped to look at the view. I needed some me time after that fall."

"Understood," Terry chimed in a little too quickly.

Chapter 55

Andy's last trip up the chair lift did not involve any conversations about impending rain. So, it was safe to say that Renee was not hip to his predicament. He had not had to pick her up from the hotel either. In all the chaos of the accident, it got late and someone went to get her so she didn't feel stood up. An intern had also brought him a shirt to change into.

They talked about the date at the candy factory. She seemed genuinely interested in him and genuinely normal. He remembered her with the chocolate. She had been pleasant, if not a little nervous. Now that she was granted a second date, she was behaving more confidently.

She was way too attractive. Claire would have no trouble believing that he could fall for her. He had to do something to get her to act strangely. Claire would never believe it if he asked for Renee to be eliminated. She was the only normal one, so far; the only one that was like Claire. What could he do?

The opportunity presented itself a little sooner than he imagined.

She sneezed.

And when she sneezed, she didn't just sneeze a little bit. She sneezed, like, seven times in a row.

She apologized and said that there must be something in the air that she was allergic to.

By the time they were about halfway up the lift, she had sneezed more times than Andy could count. Her eyes were watering and she was clearly mortified.

As she sneezed and sneezed, she scooted away from Andy to the edge of the chair and turned away from Andy in an effort to distance him from the sneezes, and the sneezes all but stopped.

Andy started laughing at the absurdity of that fact, "Are you allergic to *me*?"

She looked back at him with puffy, watery eyes and tried to laugh as well. "Are you wearing a cologne or aftershave?"

"No."

"Lotion? Hair gel?"

"A little hair gel, and sunscreen?"

"Maybe it's the sunscreen?"

"That is a pretty violent reaction to sunscreen," Andy offered. "Do you have allergies?"

"Not that I'm aware of," she shook her head. "This is the weirdest thing that's ever happened to me."

"You were fine at Sees," he reminded her.

"The smell of chocolate was so strong in that factory, that I don't think I smelled anything else."

"But you were even holding on to my arm," he recalled, "So you were closer to me then than you are now."

"This is too weird," she started rubbing her nose and sneezed again, "my nose itches like crazy."

They arrived at the top and both got off the lift and went in different directions. Mark had understood a little of what was going on as he filmed them on the way up. He mentioned it to everyone and Claire had headed back down to see if the medic had an antihistamine.

By the time they arrived at the picnic, Claire had returned with an antihistamine, but Renee was so embarrassed that she just wanted to go home. There was no talking her out of it. From about 5 feet away, she held out her hand to "shake hands" with Andy, and told him she was sorry but she was bowing out. "It was nice to meet you, but I'm afraid there is no recovering from this."

She went with the medic that came up to check on her, and they rode the lift down.

"Is there enough food in that basket for all of us?" Mark asked with a laugh as soon as she was out of earshot.

They all sat on and around the blanket and shared what was in the basket. There was so much food in there that the five of them were able to share a decent lunch.

Mark and Andy had taken off their harnesses, and were going to head down the mountain on the lift when Terry spoke up, "Hey, Sid and Claire, you haven't ridden yet. Why don't you take the harnesses and zip down."

"Yeah, Sid, it's a rush," Mark offered his harness to Sid. "Come on, it's really fun."

Andy held out his harness to Claire with a knowing smile, "Go on, you've earned it."

"Yeah, anything to get you off the ATV," Mark added.

Everyone including Claire laughed at that one.

Sid waved him off, 'No thanks, my wife would freak if I did something like this…" he paused…" without *her*." That got another laugh from everyone.

Mark dropped the harness on the blanket and all three camera operators started walking toward the ATVs before Claire could say anything. Mark yelled back "You two go ahead. Have fun."

"Andrew, show her how it's done," Sid called over his shoulder.

Andy and Claire didn't move a muscle as they watched the three of them each get on an ATV and start down. When they were out of sight, Andy impulsively pulled Claire into his arms and held on.

She wasn't sure how to react but didn't pull away. After a minute, she began hugging him back—enjoying every minute in his arms. It was then that he said, "I was so scared for you back there." He pushed back a little so he could look at her and said tenderly, "Don't ever do that again. I didn't like that feeling."

He let go of her, picked up his harness, and started putting it on. She stared at him for a second while he was concentrating on the harness and then began putting her harness on. When she was finished, he grabbed her hand and started toward the platform. Her heart started fluttering again and didn't stop until they'd made it all the way down to the bottom.

Chapter 56

Claire was fully expecting Mark, Terry, and Sid to be waiting for them at the end of the last descent, but except for the employees, the place was deserted. She was relieved. When they had turned in their harnesses, Claire settled up with the manager and made sure they had gotten all of their equipment. She assured Claire that the interns had cleaned up everything and left for the hotel. The car that Andy had been driving was still there so they had a way back to the hotel.

Andy opened the car door for her and she got in. "Do you want to go get food, or ice cream, or something?" he asked with a hopeful smile, and when she didn't answer right away, he added, "I need to give you feedback on the girls I want to keep, and stuff, right?"

Claire hesitated a little more and then nodded, "Yes, we could do that," she didn't want to make it totally obvious that she wanted to. But she wanted to.

There weren't many places to choose from and Claire was crossing her fingers that the crew was exhausted and had gone back to the hotel to crash. She didn't want to run into anyone, even though she did this all the time. She usually spent extra time with the guys during the process so she could get a handle on their thoughts about the girls. She had not done as much of that this time because she felt really self-conscious about how people perceived her actions toward Andy. She was feeling more than she should and was positive that everyone could see it.

"I saw an ice cream place in the little village about 3 miles from the hotel when you and I were here before."

Claire laughed and turned to him, "Well, why didn't we go there then?"

"On the way now, my dear," he said without thinking first and didn't catch what he said until he noticed Claire's eyebrows so high up, they were touching her hairline, "I mean, Claire. On the way now, Claire." And he laughed like it was a joke.

She laughed, too, like they were buddies, but inside her heart was fluttering again. This was becoming a regular thing, these butterflies. She liked them. They felt wonderful.

He pulled up to the ice cream place, and Claire looked around for any familiar cars or vans. So far, so good. She didn't recognize any.

Andy was over the moon that she had agreed to extend their alone time. Any moment with her was a blessing. They both ordered a hot fudge sundae with coffee ice cream and extra whipped cream, and sat at a small table away from the front window.

"It is safe to say that Renee and Lindsay are out." Andy thought he would get the business out of the way.

"Agreed."

Claire knew the questions she needed to ask, but she was dreading it. She already knew she wasn't going to be able to handle the answers, but she would have to pretend and put on a brave face. "So, tell me your feelings about the other three." Let me have it, she thought.

Andy knew how he was going to play this. He already had two girls in his corner that were going to make it their goal to be completely wrong for him, and Jessica was already wrong for him without having to act. It was ironic that *she* was the actress.

"I really like all three," he began, "there are characteristics about each one that are totally endearing and attractive."

Claire almost choked on her ice cream. She coughed and grabbed a napkin to keep anything from flying out of her mouth. Did he wait until I had taken a bite before making that declaration? She thought. All *three*?? Endearing and attractive??

He saw her struggling but couldn't retreat. He had to advance. "Jessica is just so bubbly and sweet. She really has a good heart. When we were at the zoo, she was telling me about all the dogs she rescues, and that she is trying to break into acting and has gone on numerous auditions recently."

As he droned on about Jessica, Claire had trouble focusing. She started to zone out. This didn't usually happen. Was this her defense mechanism? She didn't want to hear any of this. She wanted to scream.

He could see it in her eyes. She was conflicted, big time. She was fidgeting and she had not taken a bite of ice cream since he began. It's working.

"...and JessLynn is so athletic and fun to talk to, and Lissette has the most beautiful eyes." He stopped. Claire looked bereft...like her dog had died. He hated doing this. Hated everything about it, but he needed her to come after *him*. She had to have a reason to want to leave her old life behind and take a chance. James had drilled it into him that it had to be her idea. She had to develop feelings deep enough for her to want to save him from these women who were not right for him. He thought she might be almost there. Their time together had been magical. There was no way she didn't feel that way, too. She was enjoying him just as much as he was enjoying her. He knew it with all of his heart.

Claire suddenly realized that his voice had stopped. She looked up at him and saw that he was looking at her quizzically. "I'm sorry, Andy... go on."

She felt sick. This was not how she wanted this time with him to feel. She wanted the heart flutters back.

"It's okay," He backed off a little; he didn't want her to run. "Enough business for now…. So, what are we going to do for the rest of the evening? Should we drive over to the lake and look around?"

The resort was near a lake and even though she had grown up in Southern California, she had never seen it. She reached for the lifeline he was extending, "That sounds fantastic. I'm in. Let's go." She could enjoy a few more wonderful moments in his company and then when they got down the mountain, she would have to forget all about it and go back to her normal lonely life.

Funny, she thought to herself, she had never referred to her life as lonely before.

The lake was idyllic. They were able to see most of it from the car because the road circled it. When they got around to the east side, there was a look out point. They stopped and got out of the car. The sun was setting and there were so many colors in the sky. They sat next to each other on a low stone wall that kept the cars from going into the lake and watched the sun set. Andy put his arm around Claire and she rested her head on his shoulder. He didn't dare do anything more than that. If she had given even the smallest indication…

Chapter 57

Sid and Mark were sitting in the hotel lounge half relaxing, half watching for Claire and Andrew to return. They were the designated watchers. Terry had taken the first watch, and had gone up to her room 30 minutes ago. They all knew Claire's process, and so far, she had deviated from it way too much. Even though they knew the reason for her behavior, it was still unsettling. They didn't normally watch her like this. They all guessed that she was feeling differently about spending this alone time with Andrew. The time she spent with the guy in previous cycles was all part the show's success. This was why they were watching. They wanted to see if she could get a handle on it, because up until this weekend they had noticed her absence more than her presence. She was not there for some of the girl interviews. Maggie was doing *all* the editing with Bill. That was *not* like

Claire at all. She was also staying in the van during some of the shoots. She was usually right there in the middle of it all: directing. There was almost no directing going on for this cycle. She wasn't doing her job.

They had just been discussing what would happen to the show if Claire dropped the ball. She either needed to get it together and support Andrew in choosing one of the girls, or become the girl herself. She couldn't do both, she had to do one or the other. She couldn't continue what she was doing so far. She was risking a show failure. It was almost as though this cycle was going to make or break her. That was scaring them. And even though they completely supported this love interest and knew it was good for her in the long run, they were still torn because they were starting to feel like their jobs were on the line.

Mark had a line of sight to the hotel entrance and so he was the one who saw Claire and Andrew enter and head right for the elevators. He ducked his head a little so Claire wouldn't notice him there even though his presence in the lounge was perfectly normal behavior for him. He instinctively thought that she would be more sensitive about being spotted.

"That them?" Sid read Mark's sudden head ducking as a clue.

"Yes," Mark nodded and then sat back up straight. "They're headed to the elevator."

"They holding hands, maybe?" Sid was hopeful.

"Nope."

"Any body language?" Sid wanted more.

"He put his hand on her back to maneuver her around another person, "Mark offered.

Sid grunted, "Well it's something, but not *something*."

"Cryptic." Mark said sarcastically. He got a kick out of the simplicity of Sid's comments.

***

"Okay, Claire, I'll get on it as soon as I get the footage." Maggie ended the call and sat back in her chair. She had been editing nonstop for the last 2 days while the rest of the crew was in the mountains. She was a little miffed that she hadn't been able to go. She was missing everything. Claire wanted her to edit, edit, edit. She was not sure this show was going to be on par with all the others. Bill was patient with her, but by some of his comments she could tell that she didn't have the knack that Claire did for weaving the story together from three different camera angles, Sam's voice-over narration, music, and the kitchen sink. Claire was the miracle worker. Claire was the show. Maggie was not even a close fifth.

When James had asked her how it was going when she got to his house the night before, she had told him she thought Claire had lost it and that they were losing her. So far it looked like no one was winning.

"If this Andy-loves-Claire thing doesn't work, I will be out of work," Maggie had complained.

James was not concerned, "If what Andy is telling me is true, my sister is this close." He put his thumb and forefinger together so they were barely touching.

"You better be right," Maggie put her hands on her hips and then sat down on the chair opposite the sofa where James was sitting. "You have nothing to lose here. The rest of us have mortgages and hungry tummies."

"Is it that bad?" James hadn't thought of the show actually tanking.

"Claire is not herself, and the show depends on her."

"I'm sorry, love," James patted the sofa next to him, "please come sit by me. I'll kiss you and make it better."

Well, who could resist that?

***

And now as Maggie sat in her office, she wondered about her best friend. There must be a crazy war going on in Claire's head for her to be this distracted and absent from directing her show. If Claire is falling for Andy, Maggie thought, I can see why she doesn't want to be around the other girls or be in editing, watching their footage, looking for good shots, and good angles, and good lighting to make them look their best. She doesn't want to see him with those other girls in any shape or form; especially when they start getting more familiar with each other. Jessica was already overly affectionate. That must drive Claire crazy. And it's only going to get harder.

Just then on the phone Claire had sounded distant, like she was talking from far away. Not, like, physically far away, but her voice sounded like it was so deep inside her head, that it didn't sound like the Claire she knew. If Maggie had only known all the things that had happened to Claire that day. Claire mentioned nothing about her accident, or about the crew leaving her to ride alone with Andy, or their stop for ice cream, or the sunset. Maggie just knew Claire was changed. And it didn't sound good.

Chapter 58

"I haven't seen Claire for a week," Andy sat down in the booth across from James.

They were meeting to discuss what was going on, and Andy was frantic. James finally had a walking cast, and had gone back to work the week before. His leg was almost done healing. He and Maggie had just finished lunch and she left to head back across the street.

"Isn't she supposed to be directing this show?" James was surprised.

"You would think." Andy shook his head sadly. "The rest of the crew, even Maggie, assures me that she is in the building, but she is absent. We have been doing post-date interviews and I've been on two more dates with each of the three remaining lovelies."

"Can you protest or something? Can you demand to see the director? I mean, didn't she promise that she would be there with you every step of the way?"

"I have tried that. I get the feeling that they have no idea what to do either. This is uncharted territory for them as well."

James scratched his head.

"One of the girls has even dropped hints, and made sure she was overheard talking on the phone with her "boyfriend." She is trying to make like she just came on the show to be on TV and that she is almost engaged to a fake boyfriend. She is the one that I am acting like I'm the most interested in. She figured that Claire would at least attempt to save me from her."

"That's brilliant."

"If only someone would drop that hint to Claire, maybe she would show up on set."

***

About ten minutes before, Claire had happened to glance out of her office window and saw Maggie come out of the bistro from her lunch with James. She didn't see James. She watched Maggie and Andy pass each other crossing the street, and Andy enter the same bistro. Did she miss James? Had he left before Mags? That's funny. Oh well.

She turned back to her task. She had to think. Mark had just informed her that he had overheard JessLynn talking to someone on the phone and it sounded romantic. She was talking to someone she was obviously in love with. All gah gah, giggling... He quoted her as saying, "I can't wait to see you, okay...gotta go...I love you too," and then blew an air kiss. Mark was out of JessLynn's line of sight, so she had no reason to believe that anyone had heard her.

A few days before, Cindy, her make-up artist, had come to her in confidence. She was doing JessLynn's make up before an interview, and JessLynn had been going on and on about how much she was in love with Andrew, and then at one point called Andrew, "Johnny." She tried to explain that it was her pet name for Andy, but Cindy was doubtful. "I don't think she was actually talking about Andrew."

She glanced out the window again to stare into the brightness of the afternoon. An odd movement caught her eye across the street. James was walking toward the parking lot from the bistro. The odd movement was his walking cast-induced limp. What was he still doing there? She looked back at the bistro entrance and watched Andy emerge and walk in the opposite direction toward the crosswalk to the studio. Claire leaned toward the glass and tried to watch both men at the same time. She thought she saw Andy look back in James' direction, but she couldn't be sure.

She pressed the intercom buzzer for Maggie.

"Yes, boss," Maggie said over the intercom.

"Didn't you just have lunch with my brother?"

"Yes, boss. He sends his love, by the way,"

Maggie was immediately on alert. She didn't like Claire's tone. Careful.

"Did you leave together?"

Weird question; the only reason she would ask this is if she knew otherwise. Did she see Andy and James together? "No. He wasn't finished and I had to get back in here," Maggie laughed for authenticity, "you know James and his food, he ordered that burger that is three feet tall…"

I'm smarter than you, Claire, Maggie thought.

"Did you see Andrew?"

"As a matter of fact, yes, we passed on the cross walk." Maggie was positive Claire had seen all of this out her window and was hoping against all hope that James and Andy were smart enough not to leave together.

Claire paused and then said, "I need you to come in here. Mark has just brought me some disturbing news."

Chapter 59

"So, what do you want to do about it?" Maggie decided to throw it in Claire's lap.

She had just listened to Claire go on and on about JessLynn's supposed deception, Jessica's obvious faults, and Lissette's completely unpredictable and bizarre behavior.

Claire just stared at her. Maggie stared back with eyebrows raised—frozen in her question.

Which one of us will blink first...? Maggie was thinking to herself and trying to keep a straight face, when Claire's phone rang. Claire looked away and answered her phone.

I won, Maggie thought. Hollow victory.

"I can't right now," Claire told the phone in a complete monotone. "No... I really...It's not his...have you told him...I understand...I will be there in 15 minutes." She ended the call.

"What was that all about?" Maggie asked her

second question. The caller was not taking "no" for an answer.

"One of the interns," Claire looked very tired all of a sudden, and a little nauseous. "Apparently Andrew is threatening to walk off the show if I'm not there with him for the rest of filming."

Maggie almost jumped up and down right there. James must have told him to do that. "Well, you know, Claire, you are usually right with the guy every step of the way. The rest of the crew has been wondering the same thing. No one has seen you for a whole week." Then Maggie took a breath and let it fly, "*What is going on with you*?"

Claire looked at the clock and noted the time, and then sat down in her chair, put her head in her hands, and burst into tears.

Maggie walked around the desk and half-hugged Claire from behind and hoped that she would finally share her feelings. She let Claire cry for a few minutes, and then started asking gentle questions, "Is there something wrong? What is the matter? Is there something I can do?" but Claire stayed mute.

Finally, after she had finished crying, she shook free of Maggie's hug, "I just haven't been feeling well." She got up, looked at the clock, and smiled weakly at Maggie. "Could you go down ahead of me and tell him I'm on my way. I just have to clean up my face. And don't leave today without meeting with me. We have to talk about this JessLynn thing."

Maggie watched her walk out of the office. Claire is *not* going down without a fight, Maggie thought. She wished she could somehow tell Claire that whatever she thinks she is fighting, if she loses, she still wins. And even more profound; if she wins, she will lose.

***

Maggie walked into the studio and everyone was just standing around. Mark gave her a wide-eyed look that she couldn't even read, Sid was napping with his head resting in his right hand, and Terry was sitting on the floor next to her camera looking at her phone. Alice and Adam were sitting in their chairs. Andy was sitting in the interview chair looking exasperated, because Sam was sitting in the other interview chair trying to have a conversation with him. The two interns were milling about trying to look busy. Cindy must have been taking a bathroom break. When Sam saw Maggie, he jumped up and trotted over to the craft table and grabbed a donut.

She walked right to Andy and put her hands on her hips and mouthed, "good job, keep it up," then said aloud, "Claire will be here in a few minutes," and then said only to Andy, "she's recovering from a good cry in the restroom. So go easy, but don't back down. If that makes any sense at all," she said as she made a face that Andy really couldn't read.

Andy's eyes got wide. She could tell he was

bothered that Claire was upset enough to have been crying.

Claire walked in right then and took charge like that Claire that everyone knew. She apologized for her behavior and promised that from now on things would be back to normal. She had slapped herself around in the bathroom and resolved to let him go, stand up tall, and move on with her life. This show was her life and she wasn't going to let a little attraction let that go. A little tiny voice screamed at her that the attraction wasn't little, it was larger than her life, but she snuffed that little voice out with all her might.

Andy noticed a difference in her manner towards him immediately. It was like she didn't see him anymore. He was so glad to finally see her face and be in the same room with her, that it didn't matter at first. But by the end of the afternoon of filming, he was feeling her cold shoulder and didn't like it. Nothing he did or said mattered. His charm couldn't melt her today. Maybe tomorrow? If her promise was true, she would be with him the rest of the way. He had time.

Chapter 60

After the interviews the crew started preparing for the in-home dates. Andy had eliminated Lissette, so that left the final two: Jessica and JessLynn. At this stage, each girl invited Andrew to their place for dinner, and then they each had dinner at his place. JessLynn was first.

The crew was excited to learn that JessLynn was housesitting for a friend who had a rather large house in Orange County on a bluff overlooking Laguna Beach. She had permission to use the house for her dinner, so filming would be easy as pie. Usually, they had to worry about shooting in small kitchens and living rooms. This place was a palace with a lot of natural lighting and the promise of a picturesque sunset out the southwest facing windows.

JessLynn was no cook, so she had arranged for a local Italian restaurant to cater the dinner. Andy was proud of her performance so far; it was just annoying that she even had to be there. She was really playing the affectionate girlfriend role like she was born to it, but when she held his hand or grabbed his arm when they were walking; it was all he could do not to shake her off. He could feel Claire watching them and it made him feel guilty somehow. He wanted to be holding *Claire's* hand.

JessLynn kept dropping hints about her fake boyfriend when she knew someone from the crew was in earshot. Both she and Andy wondered if any of the hints had even gotten back to Claire. He had not had a chance in the last week to talk to James to see if Maggie knew anything about it. Maybe Claire was waiting to see who he preferred before telling him. He would have thought that once he chose JessLynn and Jessica, Claire would have informed him of JessLynn's "duplicity." Or maybe she had gotten over him already and didn't care one way or the other. He hoped that wasn't the case.

After the dinner, they moved out onto the patio overlooking the ocean. It really was a beautiful view. The sun was not going down for at least another hour, so Claire gave the crew a break so they could eat their own dinner. They all started chowing on the food in the kitchen. Andy and JessLynn remained alone on the patio.

"Maybe you should kiss me or something," JessLynn offered generously and then laughed, "unless you couldn't pull it off. I mean, you would have to be really convincing."

"I don't think I could," Andy looked pained because he didn't want to hurt her feelings, "no offense."

"None taken. Just trying to help," JessLynn, instead, snuggled close to him on the patio sofa and laid her head on his shoulder.

He could handle that, barely, until Claire came out onto the patio. She looked as if she were about to say something, and then with a very strained expression, excused herself and walked back into the house.

JessLynn sat up and smiled at him, "Well, that was telling. I'm a girl. I know uncomfortable, masked jealousy when I see it."

"Really?" Andy was encouraged. "I'm not sure anymore."

JessLynn nodded. "I would take advantage of that. Go. I'll stay out here." She nudged him out of the seat.

Maggie was eating in the kitchen with the rest of the crew when she watched Claire come in from the patio. Claire was pale. Maggie looked beyond her and saw the couple on the patio sofa and put two and two together. Claire turned down a hallway and disappeared. Then Andy suddenly came in after Claire was out of sight. He looked at Maggie to see if she knew which way Claire had gone. Maggie pointed down the hall.

He came around the corner and found her standing in the hall. She was visibly upset and in turmoil. He hated this. If he had known it would be this hard on her... and him... Oh yeah, idiot, you signed up for this.

"Uh...Hi," She looked him in the eyes first and then down at the floor. Why did she hate it when the girls touched him? She shouldn't feel like this, she made a promise to herself, but every time one of them grabbed his hand and held it, and just then on the patio... she wanted to scream. She was still wondering if she should tell him what she knew about JessLynn.

Andy thought it was encouraging that she was obviously uncomfortable looking at him. That meant something right? Didn't awkwardness mean that she felt something for him after all? Something she couldn't say? He was encouraged by what JessLynn had said.

He started to pretend not to know exactly why she was upset, but then thought better of it. He needed to be genuine with her, and he felt confidence coming from her confusion—if that made any sense at all. "I'm sorry. I wish she wouldn't do that. I'm really not comfortable with that amount of public affection from her."

"What do you mean?" Claire asked, even more confused. "I thought you said she was your favorite so far? Now that we are down to 2, you should be feeling more at ease."

"Look, can I talk to you...somewhere less...traveled?" he asked indicating the hallway. "I have a problem."

She nodded. They looked up and down the hall. The house was big, but there were people everywhere. Who knew when one of the crew would decide to look for a bathroom. She indicated that she thought that the den at the end of the hall might be their best shot.

When they walked into the den and closed the door, Claire walked further into the room and Andy reached behind his back and locked the door. Just in case, he thought. He didn't want anyone barging in.

She turned around to face him. "What is the problem, Andrew?"

"Andy, Claire; I asked you to call me Andy."

'Yeah, about that," Claire took one step closer and looked at him quizzically. "I know you like your close friends to call you Andy, and that was flattering, but why have you never asked any of the girls to call you Andy? Aren't you getting close with the final two at this point?"

"Well, actually, that is part of the problem." He decided it was time to tell her. He got really nervous and quiet. He hesitated, and then said, "I'm going to just lay right down on the train tracks, here."

"Oh, for Pete's sake, what does that mean?" Claire laughed and released some of her tension, "You make the craziest comments."

"Here goes... Claire, there's a reason why I don't let the Jessicas get too close and why I actually don't enjoy them touching me." He almost imperceptibly took one step closer to her.

"Really? I…" Claire noticed that he had stepped closer and she was feeling something she hadn't felt before. Nervous? The flutter was back, and her heart was suddenly beating faster. She could actually hear it.

"Yes. I don't have feelings for either of them." He took another step toward her. His heart was racing. He was feeling a little dizzy. There was no going back now.

"You don't?" He doesn't? He really doesn't? Could that be possible? He was moving closer now. She could see into his eyes. They were full of longing. For her. Is this really happening? He reached his hand out and brushed her hair behind her ear and left it there resting his thumb on her cheek; his fingers barely touching the back of her neck.

"I'm completely in love with someone else."

He slowly drew her toward him so that their lips were almost touching. She could feel his warm breath on her lips. The feeling was exquisite. Their lips touched ever so softly and he hesitated as if he were afraid to go any further without her consent. She leaned toward him and reached her hand up to run her fingers through his hair and pull his head toward hers. As their lips pressed together, they both leaned into each other. His hand moved behind her head and made little circles at the base of her hairline and up into her hair. Her other hand moved up his chest just above his heart and grabbed his shirt tightly. Time stood still as they shared the most tender, intimate kiss each had ever experienced.

From faraway they both heard, "Claire?" Maggie's voice was somewhere close, and that meant this heart pounding moment would have to end. Claire froze in place still grabbing his shirt. Their lips slowly parted and Andy moved back just enough to look into her eyes. He took a visible deep breath and with a tentative smile whispered, "I've been dreaming about doing that for weeks. I love you, Claire...I'm... I'm in love with you. I can't pretend anymore."

Claire returned his gaze and blinked. Eyes wide. Her expression was that of surprise. He...Love? "What?...I...I...how?" She stammered as she released the hold on his shirt and flattened her hand on his chest. She slowly pushed away so that their bodies were no longer touching, never breaking eye contact. She didn't want this feeling to go away, but reality began to creep into her consciousness. What was she *doing*? This was NOT okay, she told herself. She had been trying to move past this. A thousand thoughts raced through her head in the space of a few seconds about how inappropriate this was, how she shouldn't be feeling like this. She shouldn't be doing this. What was wrong with her? What was wrong with *him*? But he had said the words. The words he hadn't said before. He loved her. And it had felt so good, it felt so perfect.

"I don't want to pressure you or make you uncomfortable. You don't have to say anything right now." Andy leaned toward her and pressed his lips tenderly to her forehead. "I just needed to tell you." He backed away, never taking his eyes off of her. "I'll leave first so we aren't found together." And he was gone.

Chapter 61

Andy had done it. He told her. He kissed her. He could still smell her on his clothes afterwards and had fallen asleep on his couch because he couldn't bring himself to change. His dreams were full of Claire. He woke up late and wandered aimlessly around his house wondering what was going to happen. He had thrown his heart out there. Would she catch it and keep it and bring him hers? Or would she throw it back at him? He finally had to shower and make sure his house was presentable because tonight was dinner at his house for JessLynn.

The crew promised that they were just bringing pizza. He wanted the dinner to be no nonsense. He was a no-nonsense guy who wouldn't normally get all gourmet on his date, so why pretend. He wanted to be real. Besides, JessLynn wouldn't care. He wasn't trying to impress her. One of the camera

278

guys had said that it would actually be a refreshing twist for the show.

When they all showed up, Andy tried to get a read on Claire. Impossible. She avoided him at every turn. When she had to ask him something or speak to him for any reason, she never looked in his eyes. He was starting to feel sick. He kept trying to reassure himself that she wouldn't do or say anything in front of anyone. But that was really hard.

They filmed JessLynn's arrival. They had already filmed her leaving her fake "house" at the studio. Thankfully the studio had a façade that looked like it matched the beach house.

When they were all settled and filming their dinner, Claire backed away into the corner of the living room and let her crew do their jobs. She was still trying to figure out what to do about Andy's declaration last night. She had been floating around in a cloud ever since. He was all she could think about. She knew she was in love with him. She had figured that out during the kiss. She wanted that in her life, she had finally given in to the...

Wait a minute. What is *THAT*? She had been aimlessly looking at his desk in the corner as she half sat, half leaned on the desk chair pushed up under the desk. She was staring at a framed picture of *her* peeking out from under some other papers. On *his* desk. Even though she could only see half of the picture she knew exactly which one it was. It was the picture of James and her at her birthday party two years ago. They were both laughing. It was *the one* that she had enlarged, framed, and given to James for Christmas because it was her favorite shot of both of them. What is Andy doing with this? A thousand questions came flooding into one side of her brain and a thousand answers flooded into the other side. As her brain started to match the questions to the answers, she tried not to let on that something significant was happening in her little corner, but she couldn't help but let half a smile appear; if only for a split second. She started formulating a plan that would begin with a visit to her dear, loving brother.

Andy glanced over to where Claire was to see if he could catch her expression. It was cool and aloof, like she was bored. Great. Things were not looking good. He couldn't help but feel like all was lost, but a tiny part of him refused to give up. What was that famous saying? "It's not over 'til the fat lady sings." He was just going to have to make sure the fat lady came down with laryngitis.

***

James threw open the door totally expecting Mags and when it was Claire instead, he had to try not to show his disappointment.

"Don't weep, big brother," Claire laughed at his expression, "I know you wanted it to be Maggie, and I'm not offended. She is coming. She is about

15 minutes behind me because she had to go with the crew to take the equipment back to the studio first. Her car is there."

"Nonsense," James threw his arms around his little sister, "I am happy to see you. Please come in."

As Claire walked into the living room, she looked on the wall where she knew that picture usually hung, and it wasn't there. Nothing had replaced it. It was just an empty space that used to hold a picture, and was probably waiting for its return. Question #1 confirmed and answered.

"How is your leg healing?" Claire asked sweetly. She was trying to be as natural as she could, when she really wanted to wring his neck. She had thought long and hard on the way over about how she was going to handle him. She hadn't decided, yet, but he couldn't know that she had figured it out. He couldn't know until she decided what she was going to do to him.

"Good news there," he said with a beaming smile, "the doctor says I might be able to get the cast off earlier than he had previously estimated."

As he continued talking about his prognosis a crazy thought entered her mind that stopped her in her tracks. Hold on a minute. Her mind raced as she remembered the day of his accident. OH YEAH. It was the day of the first interview with Andy, and she had left the interview. Something she never does. Did James do this to himself on purpose? Was it some ruse to get her out of the interview so that...AHA...that explains where the computer got all these crazy girls.

Clever boy.

If this was true, then her brother had done this for *her*. Not for Andy. She couldn't seek revenge if that was the case. If all this was true, and it was looking that way, James knew her better than she thought he did. James knew Andy was perfect for her and he decided to sacrifice his own body in order to show her. Tears sprang into her eyes and she smiled at James as he finished telling her about his trip to the doctor.

"It makes me so happy that you are going to recover completely so soon," she made her tears work to prove her thankfulness for his quick healing. She gave him a big hug. No revenge for you my boy, just a few moments of disappointment. You aren't getting off Scot free.

Maggie arrived just then, so Claire said her goodbyes and left them to themselves.

Chapter 62

Maggie and James watched Claire leave and then wrapped themselves into each other's arms. It was a dreamy place to be. Both still could not believe their good fortune in finally finding each other.

James nuzzled his head into her neck and she started giggling and tried to pull away so she could breathe. He picked his head up and gazed seriously into her eyes.

"Hello, my love." Then he leaned in toward her and their lips met and lingered there until they were both interrupted by the front door opening.

"No fair." Andy mumbled as he walked into the entryway and passed them on his way into the living room.

Maggie and James looked at each other with sad faces. Andy looked like his dog just died. James kissed Maggie one more time, and then they followed Andy into the living room.

"You just missed Claire," James informed him, "She didn't see you arrive, did she?"

"No," Andy was sitting on the chair with his head in his hands. "I saw her car and waited down the block until she came out and left. I can't do this anymore." He looked up at them and grabbed his hair with both hands like he wanted to pull it all out. "I told her that I was in love with her, you know. I told her. I even kissed her, and she kissed me back."

James and Maggie stared at him, then at each other, and then back at him.

"Yaaaaaay," Maggie squealed and clapped her hands until Andy held his hands up to stop her. She and James sat down on the sofa.

"NO," he shook his head furiously, "there is no cause for celebration. She has ignored me ever since."

"Wait," Maggie said thoughtfully, "did this all happen last night at JessLynn's house? Or just now at your house?"

"Last night."

"Oh." She had expected him to say it had happened at his house. Maggie had noticed Claire at his house. At first, she was cool and detached, not like you would expect someone to act after they had been kissed and told they were loved. And when Claire left them a few minutes ago, she had been happier and a little bit emotional. Two different Claires within two hours. Something happened between Andy's house and James' house. What was it, if it wasn't a kiss and a love declaration? Or was she totally off and Claire was just detaching herself while Andy was with one of the Jessicas. Let's hope it's that.

"I am miserable." Andy buried his head in his hands again. "Love totally sucks."

James chimed in, "Andy, she was just here and she seemed warm and cuddly. She even got emotional when I told her my leg was healing faster than expected."

"Then she is saving the ice just for me. I knew this was a bad idea. I told you I didn't want to do this." He was rambling now.

"No, dude," James said, "really. It's gonna work. Give her time. Let her get used to knowing someone loves her. Don't give up. If you give up, it reinforces her belief that no one can love her."

Maggie nodded furiously, "Exactly. She needs you to be steady and unbending, and unwilling to give up on her. Just keep remembering that she kissed you back. That took a lot. She wouldn't have done that if she didn't feel something. Keep remembering that."

Andy wanted to believe them; he really wanted to. He had been so close to her so many times in the last few weeks. He couldn't get enough of her. He couldn't stand this feeling that he wasn't going to succeed. He wanted to hold her hand. He wanted to smell her hair. He wanted feel her kiss again. He wanted to look into her beautiful eyes.

He was starting to sound like a sappy love song. He now understood all those lyrics firsthand. He knew what all the poets and songwriters were talking about. Those words all meant something different now.

"If you want to think of it this way," James sat forward on the sofa, "she used to be this granite statue, and now she is more of a wax statue?" he ended in more of a question.

"Gross." Maggie made a face, "that is probably the weirdest analogy I've ever heard."

Andy managed a laugh. "Okay guys, I appreciate the pep talk, but I think I'll go back home and wallow in the misery that I've created for myself." He got up and walked to the door.

"Hang in there," James called out to him.

"We are on your side," Maggie added.

They heard the door close.

"I have either ruined the lives of two of my favorite people," James hung his head for a moment and then looked up with a hopeful smile, "Or you and I will be best man and maid of honor in a wedding soon."

"It could go either way, but I'm banking on the wedding." Maggie agreed, and snuggled into his waiting arms.

Chapter 63

As Claire sat in her office the next day, she forced herself to decide if Maggie had been in on this the whole time, too, or was this just James? The very fact that James and Maggie were now an item tilted her toward the former. Is it possible that this collusion brought them together somehow? Or maybe Maggie didn't know at first, but was brought in as an inside man. That sounded more like her brother. She hadn't noticed any strange behavior from Maggie, but then Maggie had been locked in the editing studio for the last 6 weeks.

Editing studio. Bill. She had to talk to Bill. She needed to see the footage from the beginning. She hoped he hadn't scrapped it all. She was fairly confident that he hadn't because he had told her that Maggie was struggling. He would instinctively save it for her to go over, just in case.

She walked through the door to the editing

studio and Bill jumped. "BOSS," he quickly clicked on something and got up to give her a hug. "I feel like it's been years since I've seen you."

"Bill, I have quite a story for you..."

***

Claire spent the entire day in the editing studio. After she had told Bill what she suspected about Andy and her brother, she also admitted that she was in love with Andy. She then told him what she wanted to do about it. She was put off for a split second when Bill burst out laughing, until he told her about everything he and the crew had been doing behind her back the whole time.

Claire was floored. It took her a few minutes to take in all the sneakiness, as Bill explained all the details. She was only mad for about 15 seconds and then she basked in the fact that all her friends had recognized something they could do for her that was risky, and they hadn't hesitated. But she wanted to nip this "mutiny" in the bud, so she swore him to secrecy. She was going to teach everyone a lesson. Nothing painful or permanent, but she felt they needed a little shaking up. She wasn't just going to play right into their hands. Bill resigned himself to being a double agent if it the end result would make everyone happy. He hoped he was able to pull it off.

"I've already done most of the work for you, my dear." Bill guided her to her usual chair.

Claire texted Maggie and told her that she was taking over in editing. She couldn't know that in Maggie's office, Mags was jumping up and down and doing a happy dance as she read the text.

"I'm sure my absence has made all of this easier for all of you." Claire remarked to Bill.

"You have no idea."

***

"Alright everyone, we have a few more interviews to shoot today, and two more dates over the weekend, then the finale. We are on the home stretch. How are we feeling?"

Claire had gathered all concerned into the main interview studio because it was the biggest and could host them all. The ones "in the know" looked at her and each other in masked confusion. None of them had been expecting her to take charge like this. It was like they were back with the old Claire, and they weren't sure what that meant. The rest of the crew reacted with naked relief, and answered in the affirmative. Their Claire was back.

As she watched the reactions of the Jessicas and Andy, now that she knew what to look for, she could tell immediately that JessLynn was in on it, and Jessica had no idea. Andy looked like he wanted to throw up and JessLynn's brow furrowed slightly as she glanced at Andy, but Jessica was all in—smiling and looking around hopefully. This explained so much. She would use this. Now that she was the one with the upper hand, she could feel. She could let her feelings come freely. She could relax. She could be happy. In just one week from now, she would finally let go of her loneliness. She had found someone she could share her life with. He had inserted himself into her life in such an unconventional way, that she had to admire him even more. It was tenacious, and it was quite a gamble. Even though she figured that James had been the author of the plan, Andy had gone along with it. Somehow, she didn't fault him for the deception. She completely understood that she would not have allowed him to get close to her any other way. She was forgiving in that respect. She understood herself and evidently so did her brother. She wondered if Andy knew James was going to break his own leg for it. She couldn't wait to corner James after this was over and let him have it after all. What a doof.

Chapter 64

Andy was beside himself. This was not how he pictured this. He was on his last date with Jessica. That was the only good thing about it. He didn't have to see her again after tonight. He was obviously picking JessLynn and making it look legit. Maybe he could use all this film in his portfolio. He would ride off into the sunset with JessLynn and drop her off at her house, then go home and cry. Wait, no, he would go to James' house first, break James' *other* leg, *then* go home and cry.

The worst part was Claire was right there, seemingly enjoying it. He had opened his heart to her and she was watching him cheerfully and bright-eyed dating another woman. Anytime he caught her eye she smiled back at him with the most peaceful expression of joy. Every now and then he thought he caught a hint of a secret in her expression, but that was even more confusing and irritating than the joy. At least she looked happy. He had to admit he enjoyed watching the beauty and happiness in her face. He would have to be okay with that for now. At least there was no more torment on her face.

At one point during the date—they were at an outdoor café in Westwood and were planning on walking around the shops—Claire had approached them after cutting the scene by circling the air above her head with her right hand. He had never heard her say, "cut," because apparently, she communicated with her crew with earpieces and didn't have to say it very loud. He had only just discovered this. It was genius, especially on location shots where there were so many bystanders. The cameras and sound guy blended well into the background. He didn't know why he hadn't noticed before. He had just learned to watch for her arm circling the air.

"How are we doing?" Claire asked them both sweetly.

Jessica spoke right up, "I have to use the little girl's room, if that's okay?" Claire nodded, and she got up and walked into the café.

Claire sat down in Jessica's chair, and stared right at Andy. His discomfort was so apparent that she almost told him right then, but she stopped herself.

"Last date. Do you have an idea who you are going to choose?" She tried to make her expression a combination of stoic sweetness.

He just stared at her. He wasn't sure what to say. He thought he might just as well keep staring and dare her to blink. He was almost angry. Almost.

She saw his expression change from anguish to anger and then back again. She reached her hand out to cover his, and then she slowly moved her gaze from their hands up into his eyes and winked almost imperceptibly.

His heart stopped.

Then she suddenly got up and walked back to her spot beyond Terry's camera. She had to keep him from losing it. She had seen the anger. She didn't want him to be angry, just uncomfortable. A brief second of encouragement wouldn't hurt. And she was counting on the fact that the cameras were still rolling. Unless Bill had given her away, they should still be ignoring her camera directions and catching every little bit of interaction between Andy and her on camera.

He watched her walk back. His heart was now beating again at double speed. What was that? Was she playing with him? Her expression had been tender and full of love. And so deliberate. If she had figured it all out and was getting even, she was smarter than he thought, and even more attractive. If this was true, she had every right to mess with him. Those six seconds had made him even more in love with her than he was before. A small glimmer of hope had returned.

Terry and Mark shared a look, "did you see that?" Terry mouthed to Mark since Claire was behind her. He was close enough to be able to understand. He nodded once slowly, so it wouldn't seem obvious to Claire.

Claire saw Mark nod at Terry. It was all she could do not to burst out laughing. This was hilarious. Just you wait, you two.

Jessica came back out and they moved to begin their walk up and down the streets of Westwood, which were teeming with tourists and UCLA students.

Adam decided that their body mics needed adjusting, so that delayed their walk just a bit, but then they were off.

Jessica grabbed Andy's hand and Claire flinched a little, but remembered how he felt about it and let it go. Let him be self-conscious for a little while longer. But then she noticed that Andy took Jessica's hand and put it in the crook of his arm instead. A little less familiar. A little less affectionate. He did that just for me, Claire thought.

As the crew followed behind—with two cameras in front—they were all able to hear the couple's conversation. Maggie and Claire were walking side by side. Andy was telling Jessica about some of his college antics including his job at the Mexican restaurant they had just walked past. "I met my best friend in college working here. We ended up being roommates and are still best friends."

"What is his name?" Jessica asked.

"Jame...Jimmy." Andy stuttered.

Maggie had been drinking from her water bottle and started violently coughing.

Claire struggled not to smile. Two confirmations for the price of one. Now she knew that (1) Maggie at least knew that James and Andy were *good* friends, and (2) she probably knew all about what was going on. She wondered briefly why she had never met Andy before if James had known him this long. She turned to Maggie to try to help her. Maggie had stopped walking and handed Claire the bottle and doubled over with her hands on her knees while she coughed.

Claire waved at the crew to keep going, and stayed back with Maggie. "Are you okay?" as Maggie finished coughing out the water she had inhaled.

"I'm...good...oh...man...that...(cough cough)..." Maggie grabbed the bottle back from Claire and took a long drink. As she gulped, she tried to think of a legit-sounding reason why she would have choked right then. But Claire didn't ask.

"Slow down, girl," Claire patted her on the back.

Chapter 65

"And then I just started choking and coughing," Maggie was actually laughing now, but in her laughter, she reassured them both that it was no laughing matter.

"You said my name?!" James got up and started pacing. "NICE. I mean, NICE. She's coming for me now. I need to move away. Far away." He looked longingly at Maggie, "I can come stay with you, right?"

"Ah, no, babe," Maggie was still laughing. "I'm not far enough away...and she would look for you at my place first."

"We can't be sure she put that together." Andy offered. "There are lots of guys named James."

"You changed James to Jimmy too fast, and then I choked," Maggie put her hands on her hips. "Claire is wicked smart."

"We are all toast." James sat back down and

looked defeated.

"If she knows, then that explains her behavior somewhat," Andy sat down and relaxed back in the chair. "It explains why I feel like the mouse that was caught by the cat, and the cat is just playing with it until it eats it. I'm just waiting to be eaten."

"But she gave you that look at the table *before* you slipped on James' name." Maggie sat down next to James in her usual place.

"Oh yeah," Andy admitted as he closed his eyes. "I have no clue. The mental energy I have expended during the last few weeks has drained me. I feel like I've aged ten years. I can't think anymore. I just want this to be over."

James put his arm around Maggie and she rested her head on his shoulder.

"What is next, Maggie?" Andy asked. His eyes were still closed.

"Well, tomorrow is a day off because Claire needs to edit the stuff we have so far to see if she needs to add anything for continuity. Then Tuesday we will shoot your final interview when you talk about the pros and cons of both girls and then we schedule the finale, which is where you declare your love for the woman you have chosen. We usually do that at a villa out in Malibu, but Claire hasn't had me book it, yet, so I don't know what she has planned. Maybe she has a different idea for you."

"Great. Something different for me…
Naturally," Andy opened his eyes to the snuggling

couple across from him and got up. "Well, thanks for nothing guys."

Maggie and James tried to reassure him, "It will be okay. Just a few more days."

Chapter 66

Andy sat under the lights. He felt like he was a suspect in a murder investigation and was sitting in the interrogation room waiting for the police to come in and rake him over the coals. He was sweating. The make-up girl was earning her money today. She had even asked him if he was alright. He had just feigned nervousness. He really felt sick. He had answered all Sam's questions as best he could. He was honest with his evaluations of the two girls, trying to be a gentleman. He had come to genuinely like each one of them. He could see how this show was so successful. Claire was really good at orchestrating the situations in which he interacted with each girl. Her crew was adept at staying in the shadows just enough to catch everything but not be in your face. The only thing he didn't like was he could tell that the cameras never stopped, even when Claire would tell them to cut and twirl her hand in the air. They were always pointed at him even when everyone appeared to be resting. He had just begun to notice it in the last two weeks.

Correction. There was one other thing he didn't like. Sam was the most annoying person he had ever met. He couldn't imagine how he was liked by fans. That had to be an exaggeration. *I could do his job ten times better*, he thought. Sam was barely tolerated by some of the crew. Andy had overheard some of them complaining about him more than once. He wished he could tell Claire, but he felt like she wouldn't pay attention at this point. She had steered clear of him since Westwood. He knew she was there in the shadows behind the cameras, but she never came into the light.

He made it a goal to tell her about Sam after this was all over, and offer his services as a replacement. Maybe if they worked together, they could start over and develop a friendship that could evolve into….

He was grasping. Desperate. Sweating. Hot. Uncomfortable. He just wanted to get out of there. According to Mr. Annoying, they were almost done.

"Alright now, Romeo, tell me again about your thought process," Sam smiled wickedly at him. "How are you choosing your forever love?"

Andy wanted to scream, "STOP CALLING ME ROMEO!" Instead, he took a deep breath and said calmly, "I don't feel like a Romeo right now, Sam. I'm going to disappoint a lovely lady that I have come to really like and appreciate as a good friend. It isn't something that I am looking forward to."

"So, you already know who it is?"

"Yes, Sam, I do."

Claire watched Andy squirm from her director chair behind Terry. He is going to choose JessLynn because she's in on it. She had told Sam not to hold back. She knew he could be annoying, and she wanted to see how Andy would react to his manner. So far, he was rising to her expectations. He was a gentleman. He was thoughtful, and respectful, but how long could he last under Sam's caustic unpredictability. This was the only time she was semi-happy with Sam's performance. She needed to start looking for a new "host."

"OOOO," Sam sat forward in his chair gleefully, "Who is it? Can you give us a hint?"

"No, Sam, I'm not comfortable with that. I wouldn't want to hurt anyone's feelings prematurely. That's just not nice."

"But she will be devastated in a few days. Why not soften the blow?" Sam wasn't giving up. "Come on, Andrew, tell us now, then you won't have to see her face, or hear her blubber and cry. It's easier this way."

"I don't want her to find out from me on TV, I want to be able to tell her face to face, so I can..."

"It's JessLynn, isn't it?" Sam interrupted, "You are choosing JessLynn, right?

Andy stared at him, and was grateful that this interview wasn't live. He got up and removed his lapel microphone and reached behind his back to remove the mic transmitter from his belt. He never stopped looking straight at Sam. Once he had set the mic apparatus on his chair, he stood right over Sam and said very quietly, "you are perhaps the rudest person I have ever met," and then walked out of the studio without looking at anyone else.

He didn't hear the crew applaud once the studio door shut behind him. It was a sound studio after all, and therefore soundproof. He also didn't hear multiple crew members yelling at Sam for his behavior. But most importantly, he didn't see Claire's expression, and she made sure no one else saw it either. She used the distraction of the attack on Sam, to collect her emotions before saying anything. She was proud of Andy. He had done exactly what she had hoped. He wasn't going to let anyone belittle or disrespect another human being.

She called an early lunch. "Be back at one, please. I want to shoot the 'rejection,' so someone find Andy and bring him back here so we can make those arrangements. And when she said, "someone," she meant Maggie.

Maggie wandered around the hallways for about five minutes not finding Andy before she thought about going across the street. Just as she was getting out of the elevator on the ground floor she got a text from James, "Andy's at the Bistro, he wanted me to tell you."

She thought it was odd that Andy hadn't texted her directly. Maybe he was afraid she would be standing near Claire and Claire would see it.

Before she even made it to the table where Andy was sitting, he jumped up, "That man is the most infuriating human being on the planet!" He was obviously still angry. "How does Claire put up with it?"

"Claire has been trying to find a blatant excuse to let him go." Maggie agreed, "I think she just found one."

They sat down and Maggie ordered a burger to Andy's surprise. "Claire called an early lunch. I'm starving. You hungry?"

Andy laughed, "Yes, ma'am," and then added, "You know...I could do Sam's job."

Maggie remembered, "Oh yeah, you are a struggling actor..." She smiled funny. "Claire hates actors."

"James already told me to keep that part quiet." Andy looked at the menu, "And I'm not struggling." He ordered a turkey sandwich.

Maggie got out her phone and texted Claire that she had found Andy and that they were at the Bistro. "I have to tell Claire where we are. She wants to shoot the 'rejection' after lunch, so you have to tell Claire which girl needs to come in after lunch so you can tell her she's not your choice."

A text came back from Claire telling Maggie to order her a turkey sandwich and that she would be right down.

"She's on her way. So, gather your thoughts." Maggie smiled at Andy. "It's almost over."

"Well, I'll admit to you that I will be choosing JessLynn. She has known from almost the beginning about everything. She guessed. She has been playing along this whole time."

"REALLY?!" Then she looked thoughtful. "Did you talk about it on the chair lift?" Maggie asked as she got the server's attention to order the turkey sandwich.

"Yes, as a matter of fact; how did you know?"

"Just a guess, really. There was something wrong with the audio that day. We have no sound for that entire trip up the lift. The helmet cams weren't working."

"JessLynn turned off both helmet cams when we first got on." Andy admitted.

"Ah." Maggie took a sip of her water, "That explains a lot. She's a smart one."

"She's been a trouper."

Claire walked in and made her way to the table, "Did you order my sandwich?" She asked Maggie.

"Yes, boss."

"Okay, *Romeo*," Claire said with a knowing smile and a small laugh, "I just want to apologize for Sam. He's a pig sometimes."

"A pig that should *not* be on your show, and thank you," Andy nodded his acknowledgement of her apology.

"I let him go just now." Claire said matter-of-factly.

Both Andy and Maggie stared at her.

"What? Really?" Maggie blurted out.

"He has been hinting around for the last few cycles that he wants to move to Australia, so I told him to buy a ticket." Claire nodded thanks to the server for bringing her a water. "We will have to shoot the next segment a little differently. I'm thinking that maybe we can go back and isolate times when Sam has said things and dub them into this last segment as a voice over. So, we don't need him. It's more work for me in editing, but I've had worse situations to fix than this." She was talking because she was nervous. "Remember the time when that waterfall drowned out the entire dialog during the date, like, four cycles ago?"

"Adam dropped the ball that day." Maggie laughed. "But you worked magic with the couple and they came in and tried to recreate what they said. It took you guys all day."

Claire laughed with Maggie, entirely aware that Andy was just staring at her.

There was a silence that was starting to get awkward when the server approached with their lunches. "Turkey sandwich?" Both Andy and Claire raised their hands and smiled at each other, breaking the tension.

Maggie jumped in, "Okay Andrew, we need to know who to call in for the shoot. Who are you *not* picking?"

"Jessica."

Claire had thought about seeing what he would say if she told him that she "found out" that JessLynn was only on the show for TV exposure and that she already had a serious boyfriend, but she decided that he was probably uncomfortable enough knowing that he had to pretend to be in love with someone else. She didn't want to be too cruel. Her coolness was cruel enough. She didn't like doing this to him, but she had been torn up inside for weeks and that was longer than he would be. Plus, she had to think about her show. She couldn't just waste this entire cycle. Half of it had already aired. She needed him to continue the charade.

Just wait, my dear boy, she thought to herself, your discomfort will be over right about this time tomorrow.

And then all our dreams will come true.

Chapter 67

After lunch they went back to the studio and Andy changed his clothes for the shoot where he would tell Jessica that she wasn't the one. The entire crew was relieved that Sam was no longer there. Claire made the announcement that Andrew would be doing his own talking and his own commentary. He had already proven himself a natural in front of the camera. He wasn't awkward and stiff like most people were when a camera was pointed at them.

This was a surprise to Andy. And a relief. He was a little unsure of what to say at first, until Claire gave him the situation. The studio was set up like a living room; supposedly his living room. He would answer the doorbell and it would be Jessica "coming over" to talk.

"Just be natural and say all the things you want to." Claire assured him. "You are a genuine gentleman." She reached out with one hand and grasped his arm and gave it an affectionate squeeze, smiled into his eyes, and then walked back to her chair.

He had goosebumps. Her words affected him. His mother had always insisted he behave as a gentleman. He had never heard another woman acknowledge his behavior that way before. His mom would be proud. He would have to remember to tell her.

A doorbell rang.

"Here goes..."

***

Jessica handled it well. She didn't cry. Andy had expected her to cry considering her emotional personality. When he gave her a hug at the end, she whispered in his ear, "good luck with Claire." He froze. She hugged him harder and he picked her up off the floor and swung her around laughing. All that stress that had been building up to this moment just let loose. She laughed, too, and gave him a big kiss on the cheek. So, she had known all along. She *was* the actress after all.

The crew didn't know what to make of this display, but kept filming. Claire would most likely edit this out.

"Cut." Claire made her hand circles, and walked toward them.

Andy put Jessica down and Jessica opened her

arms to Claire, "This has been really fun. I'm so glad to have met you all," She gave Claire a hug and waved to all the crew.

After she left the studio, Claire eyed Andy quizzically, "What was *that* all about?"

"She said something in my ear about being relieved that it was over, so I swung her around in solidarity. I'm relieved as well. That was hard." Andy half-fibbed.

Little did he know it would be his last fib.

Chapter 68

Andy showed up the next day at the studio at 10. This was it. This was most likely the last time he would see Claire so he was a little sick to his stomach, but he wasn't nervous anymore about the shooting. He had called JessLynn the night before and they had rehearsed what they were going to do. She had been surprised that Jessica had known.

The crew was set up in the same positions as the day before with the "living room" set. Andy got dressed in his tuxedo, and let Cindy do his make-up. He didn't need much.

When he got out to the set, Claire was nowhere to be found. The crew was a bit confused, but had been instructed to go forward without her, she was on her way. Adam hooked him up to his body microphone.

He sat down on the sofa on the set and noticed

an envelope on the little table. On the envelope was written, "Andy, you must read what is in this envelope to the camera in its entirety. Word for word. Maggie will be directing until I get there. Claire."

He heard Maggie from somewhere in the darkness beyond the cameras say softly, "Quiet on set, and we are rolling." He heard someone mumble something and then the clapperboard slapped,

He sat up on the edge of the sofa and opened the envelope. Inside he found a couple of typed sheets of paper stapled together. He looked at the camera and said, "The director of Single, No More has asked that I read this to you. I have no idea what it says..." He began reading...

"I fell in love with a photograph," he looked up at the camera in momentary confusion, and then kept going.

"My best friend had a picture on his wall of a girl caught in a moment of laughter. She was the most beautiful girl I had ever seen." Andy's voice broke with emotion. "I found myself hanging out at my friend's house more and more just so I could look at that photograph on his wall. The girl is my friend's younger sister. I admired that photo for quite a while until I finally got up the nerve to ask my friend if he would introduce me to her. He told me that he would gladly try, because he admitted that he thought I would be perfect for her." Andy nervously grabbed his chin with his free hand and looked up at the camera for a moment. "He warned me that she had been hurt badly by her previous boyfriend and had sworn off love. But he still tried. When she found out that he was trying to set her up with someone, she refused to even answer his phone calls or requests anymore," Andy's voice broke again, "She was closed."

Andy stood up and started pacing in an effort to compose himself. Mark and Sid had to adjust their camera angles a little, but it still worked.

"One day about six months ago, my friend, his name is James, told me that he had an idea of how I could meet his sister without her knowing it had been arranged, but it would be tricky and a little risky." Andy hesitated and looked at the cameras and then decided to sit back down before he passed out. His heart was racing and he was feeling dizzy.

"James told me that his sister was the director of a show called, Single No More, and that I could apply to be on the show. This was the only way he could think of, that I would be able to meet her. He told me that she would get to know me if I got on the show, and I would get to know her, without her ever suspecting. I could decide if my love for her photograph translated into a real thing, or if it was just admiration for a good photo." Andy set down the papers and put his head in his hands for a moment.

The crew members who already knew about this were all collectively holding their breath wondering how in the heck Claire figured this all out, and what was going to happen next. They kept exchanging glances, and Mark noticed that Bill was standing in the back with the engineers. Bill never came to the studio. Marcus and Ethan were also there, and JessLynn was standing with them with her hands clasped under her chin and a dreamy look on her face.

"I made it all the way through all the interviews, and the final interview was with me and two other candidates, but we all got to meet Claire."

He looked up and straight at the camera, "That is her name. Claire." His voice broke again. He rubbed his eyes.

"When I saw her in the room, I knew the photograph hadn't lied to me, and when we were introduced and I shook her hand, I felt an electric current pass between us. I was more smitten than before. I couldn't take my eyes off of her. She was even more beautiful in person." Andy's thoughts raced. How did she know all of this? Did James or Maggie write this? Why am I reading this? He looked out into the darkness, searching...

"I made the final cut and became the "Single" on this show. James told me that Claire would be interviewing me for two full days with her computers and matching me to ten women that would be completely compatible to me. I didn't want to be matched with women who would be compatible to me, because I wanted her. I wanted

Claire to notice me, and to fall for me, too. I was fairly sure that she felt that same connection with me when we first met and shook hands."

"James came up with a way that we could get her out of the interview so I could give fake answers to the computer. He got himself into an accident and he broke his leg...on purpose. He figured the only way she would leave the interviews would be for an emergency." Andy looked straight at the camera and with emotion continued, "And so my best friend broke his leg for me, and for her." There was a collective gasp in the studio from all those who didn't know.

He looked back down at the papers, "the interview answers that I gave during the time she was at the hospital tweaked my computer profile just enough to generate ten women with almost nothing in common with me. I have spent this entire dating process trying to get to know Claire." Andy looked puzzled at the papers because it included some stage directions right then. "Here are some examples." He said, and then he turned and watched the monitor.

He looked at the monitor and all of a sudden it showed a split screen with him on one side and the other began a series of footage of him and Claire, which slowly edged his live image out so that everyone was now only viewing the film.

Mark nodded to himself. That is why Bill is back there.

The film started out with Claire and Andy

rounding the back of a car with Claire handing Andy a wet wipe and watching him wipe lipstick off his face and sharing a laugh, and then cut to Andy climbing over seats at the stadium to set next to her. Andy watched himself flirt with her and the part where they laughed and laughed, and then the grand slam when they embraced during the celebration. The camera had closed in on both their faces as they looked up at each other. How did they know to film this? Andy was amazed.

Next, were the shots of them looking at penguins and how he made her laugh again, and then they were serving food at the rescue mission and elbowing each other and laughing. The next shots were in the chocolate factory and Andy sucked in his breath because he remembered what happened there. He watched how he made her eat the caramel and then wipe the drips of chocolate off her face. The camera froze on the look on Claire's face as his fingers touched her lips.

The scene changed to them sitting on the Santa Monica Pier bench and just talking and laughing, then they were at the race track and Claire was jumping out of the car. The video changed to slow motion as she pulled off her helmet and shook her hair out. Then she was jumping around and running at him, and giving him that last minute high five instead of a hug.

Andy's heart was beating hard. He was starting to recognize that this was all positive. This was all good stuff: happy memories of both of them.

Hoping...

The next shots were with the sloths. Totally cute shots of them both holding sloths and giggling and laughing and sharing, and then to his complete shock, there was a whole segment of them in the car on the way home. First, they were talking, then the camera geniuses in the front seat had captured when Andy had moved Claire when she was asleep to rest on his shoulder. She had just looked so uncomfortable the other way. Her neck was going to hurt when she woke up, so he moved her to be more comfortable.

The scene then changed to the beach with his arm in a sling. The camera angles were from behind, but you could tell the obvious chemistry between the both of them. Their body language was apparent. Andy hadn't realized he had been that obvious.

Andy almost fell off of his seat when the next scene popped up. They were on the mountain when Claire had gone with him the first time. No way. James must have... He watched himself act totally smitten and in love when he was sure no one was watching. And as he watched her, as well, he could see things that he hadn't noticed in the moment. She looked at him while he wasn't watching with her face full of love and admiration. She felt it too. He thought he knew it now. He had been wondering for so long, but as he watched them both on the zipline, he could be almost certain that she loved him back.

As the scene came to an end and froze on a frame of Andy looking down at Claire as she looked up at him after they had shared that hug at the end of the final zip line. The monitor returned to a split screen and showed Andy sitting there dumbfounded. He looked a bit flustered, realized what he needed to do, and then glanced down at the paper and had to flip to the next page. He began reading again.

"I can honestly say that I had no idea that any of that was being filmed," he looked up at the camera and nodded sheepishly, "and neither did Claire. Apparently, Claire's assistant, Maggie, asked the camera operators to film what they could when we were on location. Maggie saw that something was happening between us and made sure it got on camera somehow." Andy stopped reading and set the paper down. He stood up and looked right into the camera. "That is the end of the letter I was instructed to read word for word. I will tell you right now that every bit of that is true. I don't know who wrote it, or how they knew exactly what was in my heart, but it was all true. I am in love with Claire Culver."

"I wrote it." Claire's voice came out of the darkness to Andy's left. Andy turned and squinted to try to see her, as she walked into the light. She was wearing a gorgeous red gown, and her hair was piled high on her head with little wispy tendrils falling around her face. She walked up onto the set to within two feet of him. Sid and Mark scrambled to get on either side of them to get shots of their faces, while Terry stayed put on the shot of their profiles as they faced each other.

"I wrote it last night with James' help."

They made a stunning couple. His face was full of love and admiration. "How did you figure it out?" He wasn't sure what to do.

"I saw my picture on your desk at your house." She smiled and raised one eyebrow.

She was the most beautiful thing he had ever seen. He wanted to touch her, but wasn't sure if he should, yet.

"And then everything else started to make sense: why all of the girls were so wrong for you, why you paid so much attention to me, why James had a broken leg..." she trailed off. "I made James tell me everything last night after I promised not to hurt him...or you."

Andy laughed and reached out his hands, and she stepped forward and put her hands in his and held on tightly. She was trembling. "You are so beautiful." His voice broke. His eyes full of adoration.

"Andy..." Claire started, and then hesitated. "I think I have been in love with you ever since our hands touched that day we met. I felt that electricity, too. I'm sorry it took me so long. I was just scared."

Andy was beside himself with relief and happiness. "You don't know the agony I have been in these last few weeks hoping you felt it too." He brought her hands up to his lips and held them there.

Claire stepped a little closer and looked up into his eyes, "Choose me?"

He let go of her hands and cradled her face in his hands and leaned toward her saying, "Yes, always yes. I've found you, my love." as he touched his lips to hers. As they kissed, they were so caught up in each other that they had no idea the crew was running around giving silent high fives and jumping up and down and hugging each other. Maggie was kissing James, who had surprised her and arrived just before Andy started reading.

After a minute, Claire pulled away slightly to look up into his eyes, smiled, and said, "Nobody better say 'cut.'"

"Only you can do that," he laughed as he touched his forehead to hers. "And by the way, Miss Director, can I get a copy of that shot of you taking off your racing helmet in slow motion. That was the hottest thing I've ever seen."

She blushed and nodded, then her eyes widened as she remembered something, "By the way, do you want a job? I need a new host."

Andy grinned, and wrapped his arms around her waist, picked her up to twirl her around, and kissed her again.

The End

ACKNOWLEDGEMENT

A big Thank You! to my talented friend, Tucker Boyes for the cover art.

ABOUT THE AUTHOR

Jennifer Goodman raised four children, and is a grandmother of one (so far). She teaches middle school language arts at a private school in Southern California. She enjoys jigsaw puzzles, watching Dodger games, and doing 16-square sudoku.

Check out another book by Jennifer Goodman:

Influenced – A modern retelling of Jane Austen's *Persuasion*

Made in the USA
Middletown, DE
25 January 2022

59598730R20179